# METAL ANGEL

RINGS OF THE INCONQUO, BOOK 3

A.L. KNORR

AAARON D. SCHNEIDER

Edited by

NICOLA AQUINO

Edited by

BRIAN CROSS

INTELLECTUALLY PROMISCUOUS PRESS

Created with Vellum

# PROLOGUE

The percussive crackle of gunfire reverberated through the stony halls.

There was a momentary silence, the distant sound of a wild laugh, then a thunderous boom. Confused screams of pain came next, each falling silent in a morbidly slow sequence. Feet pounded, echoing without direction. It sounded like a rainstorm.

Beneath his superior's abandoned desk, a small man clutched his precious tablet and frantically swiped at the screen with trembling fingers. Closed circuit video cameras featured a facility in chaos, people scrambling for exits and clogging tunnels in panic. Others showed armed security rushing forward, outmatched wolves rushing to the slaughter. He flicked past screens of raw static before coming upon a single figure standing in front of a sealed security door.

The small man whimpered, biting his lip as he waited and watched.

The figure, his silhouette wavering as though radiating incredible heat, reached his hand toward the door then through it. The door twisted and crumpled, folding in on itself like paper on fire. There was a terrific flash and the video on the screen blinked then turned to static. An instant later came the roar of a detonation, then more panicked gunfire. Screams came seconds later.

He stared at the static-filled screen, listening to the meticulous and malicious silencing of the screams, willing his mind to think of something, anything, to do.

His superior's rotund mass had emerged from behind the desk and waddled off to a waiting helicopter nearly 48 hours ago, effectively leaving him in charge. It should have been routine, closing up shop now that the asset had been awakened. It should have been simple. He feared displeasing his superior, perhaps more than death, but nothing had prepared him for this: his utter inability to manage the catastrophe ripping through the facility had driven him beneath the desk.

There were fewer screams now, and the realisation of what that meant filled him with a desperate energy. The facility was lost, that was plain. Now recovering as many personnel as possible became the priority.

Springing out from under the desk so quickly he scraped his back, he flicked through the displays with a rush of giddy hope. The evacuation team had forced their way through and cleared out the clogs in the escape tunnels. The trickle of remaining personnel stepped over limp bodies as they left the facility.

He depressed the mic application on his tablet and fought to keep his high voice from trembling.

"Redeploy to the central corridor."

The evacuation team, a small but veteran crew of security professionals, looked up at the camera.

"Evacuation's not complete," their leader growled into his headset.

"Redeploy, immediately!"

His voice sounded shrill but he didn't care. He didn't dare cross to the escape tunnels without cover. That man-shaped thing needed slowing down. Silently, he cursed himself for not coming to this decision earlier.

"Redeploy! That is an order!"

Training kicked in. The evacuation team, slowly, began to shoulder past the last few stragglers.

Hugging his device to his chest, he left the office overlooking the pit full of cooled slag, wincing as his shoes clanged on the grated walkways. He reached the security door at the rear of the central corridor and paused to swipe through the video feeds. He watched the evacuation team filing in, weapons at their shoulders, securing the long tubular room. Their point of ingress was his target, the quickest way to the escape tunnels.

He swiped twice more and saw the same silhouette now striding toward the vault-like portal to the central corridor. He had moments, maybe only seconds.

Steeling himself to bolt across the room, he opened the door and began to run.

Three steps through the door, something clubbed him hard across the side of the head. He went tumbling to the floor.

"Get down, you idiot," a rough voice snarled.

One of the evacuation team crouched over him, a hand pressing his chest down. His vision wobbled, but between tremulous angles, he could see the door he needed. He tried to rise, but his body wouldn't. The man pinning him had him beat by twenty or thirty kilos.

"Almost got in our line of fire," the security brute hissed. "Could've gotten yoursel—"

The chamber witnessed its first dawn as the main corridor's entryway erupted into a miniature sun. Stabbing light preceded a wave of heat and shrapnel that had every man in the room screaming in pain and terror.

Blinded, his skin blistered under the caress of such intense heat. The torrent of destruction rolled over him in a series of waves, but by luck or fate he was spared the worst of it as the evacuation team member crumpled on top of him.

A few seconds after the searing heat passed, he wriggled and squirmed out from under the dead weight, struggling for breath as his sense of hearing came back by degrees. His vision was obscured by multicoloured spots, but he heard the now familiar sounds of firearms discharging and men screaming.

Crawling on hands and knees, he guessed the direction in which the door most likely lay. Despite being out from under the corpse's weight, he still struggled to breathe. In a distant, quieter portion of his mind he wondered if superheated air had compromised his lungs, or raw terror was just making him hyperventilate. Regardless, he was winded and gasping by the time his fingers struck the far wall.

His hands pawed across the walls in every direction, but there was no door.

Searching frantically, willing the shimmering distortions to disappear, he heard himself begin to gibber and mewl. His hearing, having returned quicker than his sight, told him the gunshots had ceased, and only a few men were still screaming. As his vision returned reluctantly, he could just make out the details of the wall before him. He gave a sob of relief as he spied the door. Scrabbling, he flung himself forward and shoved it open.

He lunged forward but gave a cry as he was wrenched backwards, one hand still wrapped tightly around the latch bar. He pulled and twisted, but his hand remained stuck fast and the door refused to close. Confusion bubbled through blind fear, and he looked down to see the metal of the bar had warped around his hand, while the door's hinges had become snarled chunks of steel. He screamed, hammering and pulling until his knuckles split and his bones popped, but he remained trapped.

The dread presence loomed behind him. Dropping to his knees, he contorted to beg for his life.

"Please," he whined, then words failed him at what he beheld.

It may have once been a man, slight and dark-featured, but the twisted mass of molten metal throbbing in its chest was something no mortal could bear. Glowing like forge fire, tendrils of iron, veins of bronze and runnels of lead seethed in endless loops through the bare chest and abdomen. Eyes bright beyond enduring glared with demented intensity from above the tortured body.

The small man trapped at the door heard a high pitched whine escape his throat even as he felt his tongue clinging to his lower jaw.

*KILL IT*

The voice thudded against his sense like a hammer blow.

"I want information first," the abomination said with a rough, but very human voice. "I need to know what they did here."

*KILL IT*

The demand was just as brutal as before, but this time he could tell it came from inside the horror before him.

"P-please," he sobbed again and held up a placating hand. "I-I can help you. I c-can be useful."

The abomination turned dark eyes to consider him, lip curling in disgust.

"I know you will." He laughed, the bitter sound echoed oddly with the pounding, grinding presence inside his body. "You are going to tell me everyth—"

The horrible creature's voice failed, and confusion twisted across the sneering expression. Shaking its head, the gaze refocused. It continued.

"I want to know what happened here. Tell me ever—"

Again, almost like it had forgotten what it was saying, but this time, the hellish engine sounds heightened in pace and intensity.

*TRAITOR!*

The invective was like burning poison and he threw his arm over his head in a vain attempt to cover both ears.

"Not now," the abomination snarled, face twisting with pained effort.

*TRAI—*

Its whole body trembled, then its eyes closed.

The small man knelt there, quivering, arm draped over his head. He didn't dare say anything or even attempt to free his hand again. Drawing any attention to himself seemed like a terrible idea.

"Please, try not to move," instructed a lower, softer voice from its lips. Its eyes, once dark and smouldering, were now glimmering and grey, like silver coins.

With stiff, angular movements, it reached out, touching the door. The bar flowed away from his hand like water. Clutching his liberated hand to his chest, he stared up at the transformed creature.

"You should run now." Its voice was gentle, even sad. "But not that way. They already weakened those tunnels before entering the facility. Your comrades are either dead or soon will be."

He stared down the doomed escape passage and back to the suddenly transformed thing.

"Where should I go?" He didn't care how pitiful his voice sounded.

The abomination made to shrug, but it was a sharp, painful motion, like a momentary seizing. "I'm not sure." The voice became softer, more distant. "But hurry ... I ... can't hold them ... much ... longer."

The furious throbbing began again, but he'd already begun to scramble up and away.

"Please ..." the voice called wearily from somewhere deep inside the horror. "Run."

He was out of the central corridor, taking a side hatch to scuttle down a ladder and into the lower, utility corridors. It was dark, the air close and stale, but every second took him further from that living nightmare.

He was in the knotted bowels of the facility before he heard the abomination's fury unleash in a massive series of crashing explosions. Stones trembled in the blackness, and he curled into a ball in that darkness clutching his ears as the terrible voice thundered down toward him with horrible clarity.

*FIND HIM!*

*KILL HIM!*

# ONE

"Prepped for entry." Whispered words came through my earpiece. "Go ahead, Ms Bashir."

I drew in a breath and punched out with the fused Rings, launching my will like a penetrating bolt. Across the alleyway, the rust streaked door flew off its hinges and spun into the yawning darkness. The rending sound of its impact hadn't even died away before the TNC security team swept in, weapons drawn.

A heartbeat later, with no resistance met and no shots fired, Sergeant Stewart cleared the point team to advance, then signalled for the rest of us to follow. I put my hand on Stewart's taut shoulder as I'd been taught less than a week ago and followed him across the paved street and through the gaping portal I'd created.

It took a moment for my eyes to adjust to the gloom, but once they did, my skin prickled with horror. This safe-house had become a tomb.

In the first room three bodies were strewn across the floor and blood streaked the walls. Through doorways to my left and right were more scenes of carnage. The door straight ahead was only a foreboding shadow.

More bodies, more blood. Men and women lying on the floor or pitched against walls. Some were dressed in casual business attire, khakis and light polos, while others bore more traditional Gandoura or Djellaba of North Africa. Whatever their dress, all their clothing was stained with crimson drying to shades of black and brown, and every last one of them appeared to have been armed.

Later, the emotional impact of what I was seeing would haunt me, but what struck me now was how ... conventional it all seemed.

We'd deployed to this corner of Morocco on word that a known Winterthür safe-house had experienced something strange and violent. Marks had insisted that this had to be Sark. Before I could think too hard about it, I found myself on a chartered plane to Fes with a team of well-armed men.

Three hours in the air had given me just enough time to wrap my head around what was going on before being thrown into a jeep, then creeping along with the team through hot, dusty streets. I'd been prepping myself for a head to head with Sark, or at the very least seeing his ugly handiwork, but now – in a building full of corpses – I found myself perplexed. These people had been shot. Bullets weren't Sark's way.

"I don't think..." I swallowed my words as Stewart raised a finger to his lips, looking stern.

"Sorry," I mouthed. The frosty glare softened and the old soldier threw me a wink before looking in to see the rest of the building swept.

With a few sharp hand gestures, he left two of the secondary or "clean-up" team with me and took the other two with him. One manned the doorway while the other motioned for me to join him along an interior wall.

In the dim light, it was hard to make out who was who. It didn't help that they all seemed to fit a similar type. Compact and muscular. None of them were big men – like Marcus was – except for maybe Stewart, who was more barrel-chested than the rest, but they all moved with purpose, power, and efficiency.

As I hunkered next to my assigned escort, his head swivelled back and forth, the barrel of his combat rifle following his gaze. His hazel eyes took everything in with hawk-like intensity, his focus never wavered. Even when he caught me studying him, he spared me only a curt nod, gaze already moving on.

I wished my focus was so tight. Now that the initial rush was over, I had time to process the smell. The intel must have been good because the bodies were probably only hours old, but that also meant their smell was fresh. Sheer determination to not embarrass myself in front of the security team held the contents of my stomach in place, but it was touch and go until Stewart's thick accent drawled in my ear.

"Right, let's get this mess sort'd."

The man at the outer door kept his vigil, but my guardian visibly relaxed, rising from his crouch to move to the doorway leading deeper into the building.

"Go ahead, mum." He nodded towards the door.

I felt as though the walls were twisting down at me as I stood, fighting to remain steady in spite of the vertigo. Nausea chewed at my stomach like a grumpy, old mutt. I managed a few steps before my foot caught on a body, sending me lurching against the bloody wall, hands out.

Pulling away, I looked down at my hands in horror.

"No worries, mum." My escort fished something from one of his many trouser pockets. Before I realised what he was doing, something damp and soft pressed into my sullied hands. In the gloom, it looked suspiciously like a wad of fresh baby wipes.

"Really?" My nerveless fingers folded around the wet fabric. I gave him a crooked smile, the corners of my mouth trembling, and began to scrub the blood away.

"Soldier's best friend." He gave a gap-toothed chuckle. "Next to spare ammunition, of course." He stroked the extra magazines with affection.

"Thanks." I looked my hands over, happy to see they were clean.

"Of course, mum." He snatched up the used wipes and stowed them in what I hoped was a spare pocket.

"Ms Bashir," Stewart's voice was a guttural rumble in my ear. "Are you waiting for an invitation?"

Embarrassed, I moved through the doorway into a dimly-lit corridor at whose end was another door. As quickly as I dared, I crossed the intervening space, grateful not to stumble over any more corpses.

In the next, far larger, room, were several bodies pushed off to one side. Blackened streaks smeared the floor. The bodies here had been dead longer.

"... most likely they wanted to wait for the others," one of the security team was saying to Stewart. "Let 'em get in and then mop up with a simple ambush."

Stewart's gaze probed the floor and pile of corpses until my guardian spoke up.

"Might be for in here, but not up there." He pointed a gloved hand back the way I'd come. "Bodies and bullet holes being what they are points to that lot having a bloody shootout."

The one who'd first been talking nodded, his brow knitting. "They're the fresher batch."

"Exactly." All eyes turned to Stewart, who frowned.

I stood outside the ring of armed men, not sure of protocol, much less what insight I could offer. Everything just looked like slaughter to me.

"Ms Bashir?" Stewart looked at me. "What do you make of it?"

Expectant stares pressed down on me. Swallowing roughly, I forced myself not to look at a patch where flies seethed, droning cheerily to one another. "Whatever happened here, it wasn't Sark."

"No?"

The question was asked without malice or accusation, but it wrong-footed me all the same.

"The uh ... the bodies," I gulped. "They've been shot. Sark wouldn't need guns, and it probably would have been, uh ... messier."

Stewart's team looked around pointedly, something like respect glinting in their steely looks.

"Damn place is messy enough," one of them said.

"So what exactly happened here?" Stewart frowned, putting his hands on his hips. "The conflict looks internal, not external."

A few of the team nodded, but my brow creased in confusion.

"I'm not following, sir," I confessed.

"It's Sergeant, Ms Bashir," he said in a slow, frosty tone. "I actually work for a living."

The significance of this invisible line of courtesy was beyond me, but I dipped my head in respectful acknowledgement.

"My apologies, Sergeant. Can you help me understand what you meant by internal?"

Stewart opened his mouth, but my earpiece gave a warning click before a sharp voice came over the line.

"Sarge, got a zed here, second floor."

"Confirmed, on my way." He moved toward a narrow set of stairs in the back of the room. "Let's hope for answers."

I watched him go, wondering if I was supposed to wait here or head back to the front room, when he glowered back at me.

"Double time, Ms Bashir, if you please," the sergeant barked, pointing up the stairs. "Or the poor bastard will be dead before we get there."

I didn't miss the smirks on the team's faces, but Stewart was a teddy bear compared to Adrian Shelton. Head up and my stride measured, I moved to the stairs.

The second storey was a single square room with large windows centred on each wall. There were two bodies by the southern window, one of the corpses maintaining a rictus grip on the lip of the windowsill.

Another form lay near the centre of the room where a member of security stood, weapon pointed down. Two tables fitted into an L shape stood behind the pair, bowing under the weight of monitors, computer towers, and printer-scanners. Scattered among the tangle of requisite wires and cords were several mobile phones, from modern smart-phones to something that looked like a brick with an antenna attached. All was in disarray, and as we drew closer, I could see that they were covered in blood.

"Been secured?" Stewart paused two strides from the body.

"Yes, Sarge." A soldier inched back from the prone form, a woman in a khaki romper and hiking boots. "She took a few, then hit her head when she fell."

Three roses of blood bloomed on her chest. Her skin was washed out and waxy, in stark contrast to the pink stains smeared down one corner of her mouth. Her lifeless eyes contemplated the ceiling, and despite knowing the kind of people she worked for, I wondered who this woman was and what her life could have been if she hadn't been shot.

"What makes her a 'zed'?" I asked, doing my best to say the word just as I'd heard it.

The woman's corpse gave a rattling cough, frothing at the corner of her mouth before the eyes slowly swung toward my face.

I lurched backward, heart bursting into a gallop, my rings raised in defence.

"That," Stewart snorted, pleased. He squatted next to the mostly-dead woman, snapping his fingers to draw her gaze.

"What happened?" he asked in a soft, neutral voice.

The woman's mouth worked a few times, strange clicking and sucking sounds issuing forth. She took a slow breath and coughed again, this time hard enough to twist herself onto her left shoulder. Stewart slid back a step, while the soldier moved forward, but the only danger was the woman smearing the sergeant's boots as she retched and hacked.

She fell back, chest heaving one shuddering breath after another. She was still looking at Stewart, but her eyelids had slid to half-mast.

Stewart frowned and was halfway through repeating his question when her lips twisted into a lopsided smile.

"The beginning," she wheezed, her voice low. "We are the first martyrs of the new age."

Stewart looked at me, eyebrow raised in question, but I barely managed to shrug. Something compelling and disturbing glimmered in the woman's fading gaze.

"Do you work for Winterthür?" Stewart asked.

A smile spread across the woman's features, all the more ethereal for her unnatural pallor. Her gaze wandered back to the ceiling, and for a long moment, I thought she'd breathed her last.

"I am a slave no more!" she gasped, her neck arching as her body trembled. "I've been set free."

Stewart's scowl deepened, but when he spoke, his voice was the same gentle prodding.

"Who set you free?"

She looked past Stewart, her neck craning with an unsettling, almost puppet-like motion, to look directly at me. The smile widened maniacally until I thought her face might split. I recognised the look in her eyes now and something icy slid into my belly. This was fanaticism. The woman was a zealot.

"The Untarnished King," she croaked. "He who was and He who has come again!"

Every hair on the back of my neck stood on end, and gooseflesh rippled across my arms despite the stuffy air. I wanted to run, to hide, but I stood transfixed by the madwoman's dying stare.

"Ninurta returns, and He will make all things new! We have begun the holy work, but He will see it done. Those who stand in the way will join the forgotten dead!"

# TWO

"What is *that* supposed to mean?" Jody Marks crossed her arms as she stood next to the window overlooking the bustling Thames. "Aside from the apocalyptic theatrics."

We'd left the smell of death in Morocco but the sense of impending dread in London was as potent as ever.

Stewart and I shared a look, his shoulders rising in a fractional shrug before he gave me an even slighter nod.

*Thanks for the support, soldier.*

"Do you want my best guess or only what we are certain of?" I shifted my weight and crossed my arms. "Because one slaughterhouse in Fes hardly seems like conclusive evidence of anything."

Marks gave me a measured look, the reflected light of the city and water turning her grey hair into a silver crown. I returned the stare, feeling a prickle of disquiet along my spine. Was I being insubordinate? Did I care? So far, there was no clear-cut hierarchy, just Marks offering to let me be a part of things and me taking every opportunity she offered. We had yet to determine if we were allies or if I was an employee.

"Whatever you feel appropriate, Ms Bashir." There was no challenge in her voice, but her watchful gaze never faltered.

Marks may have swooped in to save us when Daria came knocking at Museum Station, but neither of us were operating under the illusion that she didn't have an angle. The question I still hadn't answered was exactly what that angle was.

"My best guess is that in some form, Ninurta has woken," I said. "That kind of fanaticism is one hundred percent cult of personality, and you can't have that without a person to rally around. Some are falling in line, some aren't, and that's causing ... issues."

I remembered the buzz of flies and the smell of blood and had to repress a shudder.

Stewart's gaze shifted to me.

"What do yeh mean, 'in some form'?" His Highland accent was much thicker outside of the clipped communication in the field.

"They need a person, but that doesn't mean Ninurta has physically woken up. Kezsarak could attack me in dreams, and he was imprisoned, so I can only imagine what a being as powerful as Ninurta could do. Possess a host, send out his spirit, who knows? I'm just saying his mummified body doesn't need to be shuffling around for him to be a threat."

"Clearly," Stewart grunted, his expression incredulous.

I shook my head, hands raised, as I fought to keep irritation out of my voice.

"I'm not an expert in this stuff." I pushed aside a pang as I remembered the one who was. "Just keeping our perspective broad, as it were."

Marks nodded before turning smartly and taking three long-legged strides to her desk. She didn't sit but bent to tap a few keys on her keyboard then swipe at her computer.

"Either way," she said as she straightened. "It would appear that the Group of Winterthür's operations are highly vulnerable at the moment, an opportunity we can't waste. We took the intelligence you brought about Iraq and combined it with some operational data collections to come up with your next target. A brief is waiting in your ops folders for review."

Stewart nodded, but I found myself confused.

"What 'operations folder'?"

"That is something we need to talk about," Marks said as she came around to the front of her desk. "However, I don't think the sergeant needs to be here for that conversation."

She nodded to Stewart, who gave a curt "Ma'am" to both of us before literally marching out of the office.

"If that man ever smiled, I think his whole face might crack," Marks observed, eyes twinkling as she watched the old soldier depart. We shared a half-hearted laugh, a failed attempt to defuse the growing tension. There was a drawn-out moment as she studied me, and I did my best to look determined to wait her out.

She spoke the second before I cracked.

"Our relationship thus far has been ... vague." She leaned back on the front of her desk. "While I am eager to continue working with you, the reality is that I am part of an organisation, a hierarchy, and your role within that framework remains undefined."

We were on the same wavelength after all.

"I thought we were allies." My fists slid to my hips. "Partners in the fight against Winterthür."

Marks nodded. "Ally? Partner?" Her manicured nails drummed against the desk. "Yes, but unfortunately, The Nakesh Corporation needs something more official, more concrete."

On some clerical instinct, my gaze slid under her arm to spy an open folder where pages of typed text sat with tell-tale signature lines stretching along the bottom of the paper.

"A contract?"

"Yes." Her eyes intent, her tenor unruffled. "A contract to secure your position and protection as an employee of The Nakesh Corporation. It would not change the objective, hunting Ninurta and the Group of Winterthür, just connect you more distinctly to the organisation."

I kept my face neutral, though an intense curiosity to read the document surged to the fore.

She drew the folder together with one hand then held it out. "Please, peruse what we are offering you and consider what we could accomplish together. I understand a lot has happened already, but we are quick to retain the services of fantastically talented people. After all, Ninurta does present an extraordinary threat. Having extraordinary people is the solution."

I took the papers, feeling her eyes on me. "May I ask a few questions?"

"Of course." Marks broke eye contact as she moved to slide into her chair behind the desk. "Though I imagine some of your questions may be answered by what is in that folder."

I laid my hands flat against the heavy, smooth stock, weighing my words carefully.

"TNC is a multinational organisation that combats a cabal of occult villains in a secret war worthy of a comic book." I hoped the comparison didn't strike her as crass. "Isn't legal paperwork ... I don't know ... mundane?"

Marks steepled her fingers.

"The Nakesh Corporation may be part of the fight to save the world, but we still have to file taxes, compensate our employees, and manage workplace conflicts. For such mundane realities, mundane paperwork helps the machine run smoothly. After all, that is why the bloody stuff was created in the first place." She smiled.

Fair enough, but the minutiae of how to fund a corporation who spent its time and assets saving an ignorant world niggled at me. I set that concern aside for the moment and chose to use her words as a springboard to my next question.

"Speaking of employees and workplace conflicts," my stomach twisted a little as I watched for her reaction, "Will I be an employee of TNC, and if so, do I answer to you?"

Marks nodded slightly, as though working her way toward a conclusion.

"Yes. And, after a fashion, yes." Her tone was disarmingly matter of fact. "You would be an employee and operative of TNC, holding a generously compensated position. Again, read the contract."

The folder suddenly seemed heavier and I had an itch in my fingers to see exactly what well compensated meant. I beat the urge back by doubling down on the remainder of my question.

"How would I be answering to you "after a fashion"?"

The steepled fingers intertwined and folded into a delicate collection of polished nails and well-moisturised knuckles.

"Every one of our operatives functions under strategic fiat and tactical fidelity. You choose the missions you participate in, but once a mission has commenced you must adhere to the methods and dictates of your superiors. This ensures two things: that our operatives only take missions they're invested in and there is a clear chain of command. As the Director of Operations in this region, I am the one holding that chain."

This seemed reasonable, and better than what most would have expected, but I couldn't escape the reality of what she was talking about.

"So once I sign this, any mission we execute together, I'm on your leash?"

Marks' eyes tightened, but then she threw me a dazzling smile and gave a short laugh.

"Very clever, Ms Bashir. I prefer to think of myself as a coordinator. I am here to make sure the best people for the job are where they need to be so that things get accomplished and everyone comes home safe. If that takes exercising authority, it's a small price to pay."

I was having a hard time not being impressed by the smooth and sensible responses Marks was offering, but I felt certain this next question was going to be the linchpin.

"What happens if I don't want to sign?" I punctuated the question with a sharp tap on the folder.

Marks looked me in the eye for another uncomfortable collection of seconds before settling back in her chair.

"Besides my personal grief and sense of failure?" She shook her head to dispel the rhetorical flourish. "Immediately, nothing. You are welcome to stay in our facilities until your uncle and Ms Davies can be transferred to a long-term care facility, then we will provide you with transportation to wherever you would like to go."

"And would I *then* be an enemy of TNC?"

"Of course not." There was a hint of reproof in her tone. "You would be welcome to come back if you had a change of heart, but even if you never did, no one in the Corporation would bear you any ill will."

Marks shook her head, another tight but knowing smile playing at her lips.

"We have enough enemies without making new ones of old allies."

I searched her face for deception but came up empty.

"So you'd let us go?" I was openly credulous in a desperate hope to reveal some dark agenda. "Just like that?"

Marks nodded slowly and gave me what was perhaps the most sincere look of pity I've ever received.

"Yes, Ibby." Her tone was gentle, but insistent. "It is not what we want, but as I said, we have enough work without going after those who share our interests. You are not our enemy, and we will only ever treat you with respect, but let me request that you consider one thing."

I waited for it.

"How well were things going in your war against Ninurta and Winterthür *before* we showed up?"

# THREE

"She's not wrong." I sank back in the chair as I held Jackie's hand.

Her fingers were cold and limp in my grip, gone was the warm strength she'd always had.

During every visit I took her hand and spoke to her, told her whatever was on my mind. I wanted her to know that she wasn't alone. My habit of talking out my worries and woes with my best friend wouldn't be broken, even if she were in a coma. I chose to believe she knew I was with her, understood me, felt my presence.

"I know it doesn't do any good to play what-if, but I can't help thinking that you wouldn't be like this if we'd met them earlier. If they'd showed up before we went to Pierre's manor, or even before Sark ... you wouldn't be ... well, it would have been different."

The ventilator hissed and puffed in time with the rise and fall of her chest. Tubes sprang from her mouth and nose.

IVs ran from her hands and wires connected the pads speckling her chest beneath the hospital gown. Machines gave incremental chirps as numbers and codes blinked from screens. My friend seemed less a singular person than a biomechanical ecosystem, her body the central host to a plethora of electronic fauna.

"Regardless," I swallowed around the lump in my throat, "getting rescued last-minute is one thing, but signing up with Marks is another. The woman is formidable. If you could get over your suspicion of new people, you might even like her."

The trauma and blood loss from Jackie's injuries had been extensive, and though the facilities in the floors behind Nakesh's public face were exceptional, there was only so much they could do. The trauma surgeon who had worked on Jackie told me the fact that Jackie was alive at all was a testament to her resilience. Even after working on her for hours, the best they could manage was a stop-gap. Jackie's heart was beating, her brain showed the very barest signs of activity, but she wasn't waking up, and she wasn't breathing on her own.

"I could believe Marks knows what she is doing." I shrugged, feeling a fresh weight settle over me. "But what makes her competent also makes her ruthless. We know how it went the last time we had an ally like that."

The surgeon had also told me that it was possible Jackie could wake up, her body healing enough to handle its own functions while her brain recovered from so much time with so little blood. It could happen, but she'd also told me that the likelihood that she would *never* wake up was far greater.

The longer Jackie stayed like this, the less likely her recovery would be, and, eventually, a body without a functioning brain fails. She mentioned organ failure and necrosis, such precise, sterile words for an ugly reality. Despite my hopes and beliefs, my friend could be gone even now. Leaving me clutching at a shell.

"Still, I think we can get more done with their help." I leaned forward to rest my head on my outstretched arm. "I just don't like the idea of following orders. We made it this far trusting our instincts..."

My voice trailed off as I looked up at Jackie. My vision blurred as tears sprang up and ran hot, familiar trails down my face. I choked off a sob.

The ventilator maintained its reptilian sounds while the avian chorus of monitoring machines played on.

"Maybe, you're right." I sniffed, lifting a cold finger to press against my brow. "Maybe, I need to face facts. My leadership hasn't amounted to much. Perhaps, I should give someone else's a try."

---

"ARE YOU SURE ABOUT THIS, IBBY?"

Uncle Iry sat in The Nakesh Corporation courtyard, in his wheelchair.

"*A'am,* if I was sure, I wouldn't be here asking you." I sank face down onto the little cafe table between us. I probably looked like a petulant child but I was past caring. I could still taste salty tears at the corners of my mouth.

"I can see reasons to take what she is offering," I muttered at the table. "But I can also see reasons why we shouldn't sign with a shady company that claims all its covert operations are to fight a rival secret society."

I felt a large, calloused grip settle over my hand and looked up at Uncle Iry.

"Ibby, I am not sure there is a right answer." He gave my hand a small squeeze. "We are so far from what either of us has ever known. I could tell you to do one thing or another, but it would be little more than a guess, not advice or wisdom."

I squeezed his hand back and propped myself up on my other elbow.

"At this point, I'll take guesses as well as I'd take advice. Though, only one per customer."

A smile crept across his weathered features, the lines in his face deeper and more numerous than ever.

"Well then." He gave a small groan as he sank back, releasing my hand. "I better make it a good one."

I crossed my arms, leaning on both elbows, feeling a little younger, a little lighter as I waited for the advice of my elder. He claimed only to guess, but Uncle Iry was the voice of wisdom in my life. His patience, his perpetual refusal to surrender to the bitter difficulties he had endured, his gentle way of speaking truth, all bound into one beautiful soul. The guesses of Irshad Bashir were worth more than a legion of wise men.

"What should I do, *a'am*?"

Uncle Iry glanced around, the little courtyard ringed in brilliant flora on stake trellises that nearly butted up against the glass windows of the complex. He looked up, squinting as the sun glittered off the dozens of floors worth of windows as they stretched into the sky. Finally, he looked down at the wheelchair where one leg rested on a pedal while the other stretched in front, encased in a cast from calf to mid-thigh. The cast stabilised the femoral break he'd suffered when Sark betrayed us and Daria destroyed spectral Museum Station. The doctors, furnished by TNC, had been optimistic about his recovery with nearly full functionality, which was fantastic given the severity of the break. In the overwhelming first few days at TNC it had been welcome news as Jackie's situation had been so touch and go.

"All of this is concerning," Iry finally said, waving a hand to the courtyard and the massive office space around us. "It is all an illusion, a mask hiding a group of people who live very differently from those who walk by this building."

I opened my mouth to point out they couldn't hang a sign on the front door saying WE FIGHT BAD GUYS, but my Uncle's raised hand stopped me. I'd asked him, so I should let him have his say.

"I understand." He nodded slowly. "They have good reason to keep secrets, but men who are good at keeping secrets are also good at making more secrets. They breed them, as a shepherd breeds sheep, so I can't help wondering what other secrets they have. There could be atrocities hidden behind those shiny windows, and we would never know."

I could see his point. With the painful exception of Sark, everyone else in our little band of fighters against Winterthür had been people we knew and trusted. Jackie was my best friend, Lowe a mentor bound by blood and destiny, and Uncle Iry was the only living family I had left. Even Marcus, the latecomer, had been co-worker and friend, who'd gone above and beyond to save me. TNC had none of that going for them, and even in the few weeks since they rescued us, it had been clear there was much going on.

"We can't trust them." I felt a decision solidify in my mental grip. "So, how can we put our lives in their hands?"

Iry gave me a side-long glance. "Hold on now." He wagged a finger. "I wasn't finished."

I threw my hands in the air. "*A'am,* please! Put me out of my misery."

"Impatient child," he grumbled with hollow derision, the corners of his mouth twitching up. "Listen longer and speak less, especially when you ask for advice."

I rolled my eyes and then shot him a sly look. "I thought this was just a guess?"

"Don't change the subject." He made a show of adjusting the wheelchair's seat. Once he was done, he reached down and tapped a finger on the plaster on his leg.

"This is what gives me pause." He hooked a thumb over his shoulder toward the doors which led out of the courtyard, to the elevator down to the medical levels. "Also, the care they are taking with Jackie. Both suggest that these secretive people might be diamonds in the rough."

I didn't rise from my slouched position, but I watched my uncle intently, snatching up every word like spilled treasure.

"We have had to trust them for many days now. What do we have to show for it?"

A small, ugly voice inside me wanted to make a snide remark about Jackie's condition, but I snuffed it out on principle. I couldn't lay the blame for my friend's injuries at the feet of TNC. It was Daria who'd been responsible for that. My molars ground together at the thought.

"If this woman--Ms Marks—is as nefarious and ruthless as we imagine she could be, why would she go to all the trouble of tending to us? We could have died under substandard care. In truth, she could have had us killed, and it would be unlikely you would have thought it was anything except our injuries, Jackie especially."

The thought made me shiver and wrap my arms around myself. Two of the closest people I had, gone in one fell swoop ... my heart lurched in my chest, grateful things had not turned out that way.

"Free of people to care for and looking for revenge, she could have used your rage and grief to turn you into a weapon. Blinded by loss, Marks could have set you after every enemy she had, and you would have destroyed them without a second thought. You have your father's eyes, but your mother's fire, and that fire fed by a broken heart could burn down the world."

Again, I knew what he was saying was true, but the thought of it unsettled me. I remembered the rage I'd felt when Sark had first taken Jackie and then my fury when facing Pierre.

I'd never thought of myself as an angry person, and maybe I wasn't, but there did seem a deep reserve of wrath somewhere inside of me. If I had lost my uncle and my best friend, what kind of person would I have become?

"But she didn't do that." I shook off the layers of dread and refocused on the facts. "So she's one of the good guys?"

Iry shrugged, and the lines in his face deepened again as a pensive frown settled over his features.

"Maybe," he sighed. "Whatever her intentions, it's clear she values you. She is a strategist or she wouldn't be in the position of power TNC has put her in. She knows helping us puts you in her debt, but she wants that debt to be honoured by someone powerful, someone she can leverage. In time we may find out if she's worth trusting, but presently, she is playing a long game, and that is good for us."

I took a minute to digest this, doing my best to set aside how guilty I felt every time I looked at his leg. Guilt wouldn't mend his leg, but the right choice now could ensure such injuries--or worse--didn't happen in the future.

"So you think I should sign up with Marks? Is that what I'm hearing?"

The words had the weight of finality as they fell from my lips.

"I cannot make that decision for you, Ibby. But if I were you, I would consider following these bread crumbs to see where they may lead. We have found a powerful ally—until we see evidence that they are otherwise--and in these times we can use all the help we can get." Iry stifled a yawn. Dark pockets of weariness had sprouted under his eyes. "Before you go, could you help a babbling old man back to his bed?"

I pressed the lump in my throat aside and put on the best smile I could manage.

"Of course."

# FOUR

Signing on with a secret society was far less esoteric than I'd imagined. More like signing a lease for a flat. So many little spots to review and initial, so many places to sign and date, but once I was done I was given a key card, an account and access to the company networks, and the promise that my salary deposit would be made post-haste.

That final thought put a bounce in my step as I walked out of Marks' office: well compensated, indeed! My sprightly mood lasted until I reached the elevator, where I was intercepted by Corporal Bordeaux, one of the security team members.

If there was anyone who could match Stewart for the grim stare down award, it was Bordeaux, whose features looked chiselled out of granite. The only sign he was really human was a long jagged scar across his neck, where the words "*par le sang versé*" had been inked alongside the old wound. Flinty black eyes glared from beneath heavy brows, and my cheer shrivelled rapidly.

"Stewart wants you for a briefing," he informed me with a voice like raw gravel.

Bristling, I eyed him. I'd just signed up, and I was already getting ordered around?

"Right now," he barked, making me jump. "Stewart wants you present for the briefing on the next operation."

"The terms of my contract is fresh in my mind," I growled, narrowing my eyes throwing some sass into my hip. "*I* get to choose what operations I do and don't take."

Bordeaux's expression didn't budge, but an intense, almost feverish light came into his eyes. When he spoke, there was an eager edge to his grinding voice.

"Trust me; you want in on this one."

My defiance reluctantly crumbled at the gleeful undertone in his words. Curiosity raised its head. "Really?"

"Yes, ma'am," he rumbled with what might have been the closest Bordeaux ever came to a laugh. "Weren't you the one who brought the intel about Iraq?"

---

"IT'S GOIN' to be a hard noot to crack," Stewart remarked as the lights came up in the briefing room. The projection of the complex's estimated layout alongside topographic maps of the area were still superimposed on the wall next to him.

"Lucky for us, we'll be bringin' a few nootcrackers."

I thought for a second that he was talking about me, and was uncertain whether I should be proud or outraged at being called a "nootcracker". But when the security team smiled and pounded their fists together before releasing them in pantomime explosions, I realised they were talking about explosives. Before I could help it, disappointment seeped around my edges. They were excited about getting to blow things up, not about me.

"Your outfitting papers will arrive shortly," Stewart continued, pretending he didn't notice the excited muttering around him. "We're wheels up at 0400, and live by 0800, so get your outfits sorted in the next few hours and then tuck in early. Dismissed."

There were murmurs of acknowledgement as the soldiers climbed to their feet, some talking as they left while others bolted, determined to use their last few hours well before lights out.

I got up and moved toward the front of the room, where Stewart was packing up the laptop he'd run the presentation from.

"Sergeant?" I stopped on the other side of his desk. "Could I speak to you?"

He gave me an affirmative grunt as he clicked the black briefcase shut, his expression no more disapproving than it usually was.

The room had emptied quickly, but I had to shift aside sheepishly as the last gaggle of soldiers skirted by the front of the room to the exit.

"Bordeaux said you wanted me to be here for the briefing," I began, fighting the urge to fiddle and shift back and forth like a kid asking for a cookie. "So I assumed that you wanted me to be part of the operation, but I wasn't mentioned, except that Hadlynne was supposed to keep an eye on me."

Stewart let out a heavy, sonorous breath.

"You object to Hadlynne, then?" He stood the briefcase up on the table, gnarled hands gripping either side.

"No, Hadlynne is fine," I said with a dismissive wave.

"Then I s'pose I dinna ken what the issue is."

I took in a steadying breath, determined to keep my voice level.

"The issue is that I am on the team now; you wanted me in the briefing, but I haven't been told what my role is in this operation. I need clarity. Direction."

Stewart gave me a hard look. It took willpower not to squirm. Finally, the old Scot nodded and then laid his brief-case down on the table again.

"I understand what you're asking, Ms Bashir," he said, raising a hand to knead at his brow as though nursing a headache. "You're eager and powerful, but you're not a soldier. This operation is strictly soldierin' in its initial phases. You are coming along as a courtesy to Ms Marks and for experience. If you want a title, call yourself an observer, but otherwise your job is to stay out of the way."

"What about Fes?" I asked. "I opened the door and followed orders. How is this any different?"

Stewart shook his head, clucking his tongue. The dismissive gesture made my teeth grind together in irritation.

"With Fes we had good intel that most were either dead or gone." The old soldier slowed his words and softened his tone, like he was talking to a child. "This is a fortified enemy position with evidence of active hostiles. I let you show-off in Fes because Ms Marks instructed that it should be so, but now that you're part of the command structure, my only instruction is to include you. Be thankful I'm willing to do that."

A tremble of anger ran through me, and I had a petulant desire to show him the kind of power I could bring to bear. Metallic aura in the room sang in the background, offering themselves as instruments of a dramatic demonstration, one that would wipe that condescending look off Stewart's face.

"Don't you understand that I am wasted as an observer, Sergeant?" I bit the words out through a clenched jaw and made air quotes around the word 'observer', trying not to sneer the word. "Not every problem can be solved by a military solution."

"With all due respect, Ms Bashir, that's where we disagree. It's why I do what I do. Every problem does have a military solution, it's only a matter of scale." He gave me a close-mouthed smile that made me want to scream. Instead, I took a slow breath and counted to ten.

I wanted to throw my past victories in his face. One look in his eyes told me that he wouldn't be impressed, and given who he worked for, maybe he had a right not to be. Respect had to be earned, and throwing a tantrum wasn't going to do that. Maybe I needed to check my pride and let him run his team the way he saw fit. My chance to show him I should not be so easily dismissed would come, I had no doubt of that. Patience, Ibby.

"Alright." I exhaled. "It is your squad, you know best."

Stewart nodded, sweeping up his briefcase.

"Glad to hear it." He made toward the door.

I stood at the table and watched him go.

"Ah!" Stewart turned at the door, his expression that of a man remembering something unpleasant.

"That great brute you came in with, he's been pestering me and some o' the lads about comin' on operations. Almost as irritatingly eager as you."

An odd combination of defensiveness and embarrassment rose in my heart at his mention of Marcus. I gaped for half a moment, struggling to know what to say that wasn't a betrayal of my boyfriend and wouldn't rouse more of Stewart's ire.

"He just wants to help," I offered with a shrug. "Same as me."

Stewart snorted, and then turned to leave again.

"Tell him to bother someone else about helping," he called over his shoulder. "Before one of my lads puts him in a bed next to your uncle."

. . .

"HE SAID WHAT?!"

I hadn't been sure that telling Marcus exactly what Stewart had said was a good idea. Turned out it was a terrible idea.

The large muscles that sloped up from his shoulders to his neck bunched into trembling knots as he ground his teeth loud enough for me to hear. The bruises from the beating at Pierre's manor had faded from sight, but as his skin flushed, there were blotchy shadows left in their memory.

"Stuck up bastards," he rumbled as he began to pace across the small common room that sat between the suite of rooms we'd been given. His hands clenched into meaty fists.

"I hope one of 'em does have a go at me. We'll see what gets broken!"

I understood his frustration, but for all his strength and bluster, he really was a gentle giant. I moved in front of him and reached up to take his face in my hands.

"Hey, no one's here now, hard case." I drew his face down toward me. "It's just you and me."

He almost surrendered, bending close enough that our lips nearly brushed, but he twisted his head to the side. My mouth grazed his stubbled cheek as he leaned forward to whisper into my ear.

"And soon it will just be me. Alone, again," he whispered, pulling back to watch the words sink in.

"What are you talking about?"

"Don't pretend," he grunted, his expression incredulous as he straightened. I let go of him, crossing my arms as I stared up into his face, forcing my expression blank.

"I'm not pretending," I lied, a keen stab of guilt driving all the way to my heart. I thought I knew what was coming and I didn't have an answer. "Could you just tell me what is bothering you?"

He cocked an eyebrow, his scowl deepening.

"You mean besides your new boss threatening to have one of his little tin soldiers put me in a hospital bed?" He snarled.

"Yes." I rolled my eyes. "Besides that."

Marcus threw himself down on a loveseat, which gave a groan of protest.

"How about the fact you signed up with Marks without even talking to me about it first? And now you're off chasing danger around the world while I'm stuck in an office-shaped prison."

I glowered. "I don't need your approval to do anything. You don't own me, Marcus."

Marcus sat up sharply, his mouth hanging open in a way that just made me want to smack him. He made an outraged scoffing sound in the back of his throat.

"I may not, but TNC does now. Don't they?" he shot back, the words sharp and hot.

"That's a choice I made," I spat, desperate to say something to drive off the sting of his words. "And you have to get used to me making my own decisions; otherwise, we aren't going to last long."

The implied threat had the desired effect as I watched Marcus's anger turn to fear, but it wasn't gratifying in the least. Instead of triumph, I felt sick, and rather than feeling strong, I felt ready to crumble. Regret moved in, hard and fast.

"Marcus ... I ..."

What was it about romance that robbed a person of the basic ability to communicate? My heart throbbed painfully at the look on his face, a look I had put there. My mouth went dry and words wouldn't come. Why was it so difficult to apologize?

Marcus held up a hand, quieting my floundering, before turning it to squeeze at his temples.

"Ibby," he began in a sad, weary voice. "I'm not trying to control you or own you. I ... I love you too much for that. But when you signed that contract, you signed me up too. That's what being in a relationship is, sharing things, sharing life. I just wished we could have talked about it."

Another needle of guilt. He wasn't wrong. Even if he had considered leaving me to face Ninurta and Winterthür alone, he couldn't go back to his old life. The enemy had seen him. He was bound to me now, like it or not, and though I'd made the choice for his benefit, I'd made it without him.

"I'm sorry," I croaked, looking down. My cheeks felt warm. "I should have talked to you; it's just... I feel like things are building. Even before learning Ninurta had awoken—"

Marcus muttered a low, vicious curse.

I blinked with surprise before I realized why… I'd forgotten to tell him about what happened in Fes. Damn it.

"I'm sorry, I was going to tell you." I put my hands out. "It's just that things have been moving so fast."

Marcus waved off the apology and then bent over and held his head in his hands.

"So that's what you found out in Morocco?" he asked. He dropped his hands between his legs and looked up, misery etched into his features. "That Ninurta is awake?"

"Sort of." I shrugged, not having the time or the energy to go over the sorry details. "It wasn't proof so much as hearsay, but I just know it's true. I can feel it."

Marcus nodded and I loved him for the simple, trusting gesture that said he believed in me.

For a moment, the conversation hung there, caught on the inescapable dread we both felt. Ninurta awoken meant, as best either of us understood, apocalypse cometh, and the end is nigh. Standing in the wake of that moment, it seemed appropriate to share a moment of silence.

"So that's what's next then," Marcus sighed, his voice catching and cracking softly. "You're going demigod hunting with the goon squad."

I almost laughed but then something hit me like a brick-hauling lorry.

What if we faced Ninurta tomorrow? The speed with which everything happened, combined with Stewart's dismissiveness, had driven the terrifying thought out of my mind, but what if Ninurta was there in Iraq? There was some underlying assumption that he was out converting Winterthür operatives, but maybe not. What if they came to him? What if I was literally walking into the lion's den with a crotchety old bully who wanted to keep me side-lined?

My knees turned watery as I fought back a shiver.

"I guess so," I said, unable to keep the quiver from my voice. Suddenly, my chest felt tight and I struggled to draw a deep breath.

Before I knew what was happening, Marcus had risen and scooped me up in his arms.

"Hey, hey, Ibby," he muttered softly as he drew me against his powerful chest. "You don't have to go tomorrow. You can stay, stay here with me."

There in his strong arms, feeling the pulsing warmth of his body next to mine, that was exactly what I wanted to do. Just stay. My contract had formalized it--all operations were voluntary. That meant I could bail even now. Stewart didn't want me anyway.

But... if Ninurta really was awake and in Iraq, I was the security team's best hope, no matter how meagre that hope was.

"I have to go." I sobbed into his neck. "I know it sounds crazy and stupid, but I'm an Inconquo. I have to go."

"It's not stupid," he breathed against my cheek, but I felt disappointment soft his frame. "It's part of why I love you. But if you have to go, then I should go with you."

"They won't let you." I pressed myself against him, hungry for his willing strength and warmth.

In response he drew me even closer, tightening those arms around me.

I knew that wouldn't be the end of it. I could practically feel him thinking, shifting through ideas and options like a dealer shuffles a deck of playing cards.

But at least for the moment, we were together.

# FIVE

"Your boy's got stones; I'll give 'im that."

Stewart's expression made it clear that he was a far way from being truly impressed.

We were en route to Iraq, TNC's plane chasing the dawn as we coasted over what might have been Turkey.

"What happened?" I cringed waiting for the answer.

I'd fallen asleep in Marcus's arms on the loveseat and woken alone in my bed as my alarm went off. I hadn't seen Marcus as I left and didn't want to wake him if he was sleeping in his room.

"Came to my quarters," Stewart said with a slow shake of his head. "Woke me up."

"Oh, boy." I rubbed a hand over my eyes.

"Stuck my service pistol in his face," Stewart grunted. "Explained with some choice phrases how I didn't appreciate the interruption. Didn't have a round chambered of course, but don't s'pose he knew that."

For a moment, I gaped at what he was describing, trying to convince myself that the thrum of the engines had confused my ears.

Stewart continued. "Boy didn't even flinch. Rare for a civilian."

I took a steadying breath, reminding myself that I was part of a hierarchy now, one I was just getting to know. The long looks the sergeant was giving me gave me no illusions as to what this was: a test. Unintentionally, Marcus had provided Stewart with the perfect opportunity to see how I handled it when my superior did something I didn't like.

"Then what happened?" I asked, flattening my expression and tone.

Stewart nodded incrementally, and I dared to hope there was the barest hint of approval there.

"Told me he would be comin' on a mission someday, but until then, I better treat you like any other member of my team. You'd earned that much, he says."

I'd braced myself to not display emotion. But what Marcus had asked of the stoic old soldier: he understood what I really valued, and in his own blunt way he'd tried his best to see it done.

Something might have blurred my vision, but I blinked it away. Clearing my throat, I held his gaze. "And what did you tell him?"

"To get stuffed, obviously," Stewart stated mildly. "I'm not going to treat some tourist as anything but what they are. Magical powers or not."

I sighed, leaning back against my seat. "Glad we cleared that up."

---

AFTER BEING REDEPLOYED from a hidden airfield by helicopters, we crept along low hills until we reached the rocky cliff face; the entrance to the compound. The round portal had two peeled wings of metal around an opening a person could easily step through.

"Sarge, this nut's been cracked," someone observed, obviously disappointed that we didn't need the breaching charges.

A corrupt, cloying smell wafted ominously from the gaping entry.

Several of the team stole glances in my direction before entering. Over the radio I heard soft curses and even a muffled gagging sound.

Once Hadlynne and I entered, we understood why.

It was an utter slaughterhouse. Bodies were strewn from one corridor to the next. Flickering fluorescents revealed one example after another of exactly how people could die, and we had to wade through the miasma of their graceless decomposition.

Through it all, beyond what mortal sense could provide, a putrid tenor resonated across my metallic sense. A creeping unease stole over me.

Something squelched under my boot, and my stomach twisted violently. Two steps later I was sick.

Since realizing my Inconquo heritage, I had all too quickly been exposed to too much violence, too many bodies. Sitting in a lecture hall back at the university, surrounded by lively, healthy students had been my daily reality not that long ago. My greatest concern then had been making good grades and dodging Adrian Shelton. My daily reality now was a far cry from what it once was and it filled me with a longing to go back in time. I'd take Adrian Shelton over this, any day. I might slowly become desensitized to the death of others, but I wasn't there yet. In some small corner of my mind, I didn't *want* to desensitize to it. Horror at the pain and murder of other people was part of being human.

Shuddering, I straightened and took a drink of water from my camel pack, swishing out my mouth. I might have been more upset about losing it in front of the team, but I'd heard some of them sharing the ignoble experience with me.

"We're a little late to the party," Stewart grunted as he trudged on, sounding as stoic and unflappable as ever, but the blood drained from his face as we moved deeper into the compound.

"Most of these died fighting," Bordeaux said, nudging a tangle of assault rifles whose barrels had been twisted together. "Or at least they tried to."

We moved down a series of metal stairs set into the stony floor and came to a rectangular room whose far wall encompassed a large vault-like door that had also been ripped open. The curls of metal spiralling out from the door were made of welded sheets of metal thicker than the breadth of my hand. That much metal could have put even our unused breaching charges to the test, but it had done the people inside no good.

"What the bloody hell can do something like this, Sarge," one of the team asked, his voice barely audible in horrified wonder.

I turned to see the muscles in Stewart's square jaws hard at work, grinding up one unspoken explanation after another. He must have felt my eyes on him because his gaze snapped over to me and narrowed with suspicion.

"Is this Ninurta?" He spat the name, as though he didn't like the taste and wanted to expel it as quickly as possible.

"I don't think so," I said, and then seeing his waiting glare added, "it feels familiar in an unpleasant way. Give me a moment."

Closing my eyes and letting my metallic sense broaden and deepen, I blocked out all other auras and drew on the cords which rose from the huge door.

I was staggered by the potent and utterly rancid presence that filmed the metal door. The unease that had been encroaching on me with every step into this abattoir swelled into a sickening certainty that I did indeed know this particular blend of corruption. It had been over a year since I'd felt its consuming, volatile touch, but in such potent quantities, I couldn't mistake it for anything else.

"It's Kezsarak." I felt my soul grow heavy as I uttered the name.

The fused rings on my fist pulsed with a pugnacious sympathy, remembering the old enemy.

"Wasn't that a demon?" Bordeaux asked, his eyes searching the ruins. "I thought they were trying to raise some kind of demigod or sorcerer-king."

"They were." Stewart pointed back towards the entrance. "But this looks like someone goin' out, not comin' in. The evidence suggests gunfire going outward. Poor bastards were holdin' the line as the devil walked among 'em."

A grim silence followed and I felt a pang of pity tug at my heart for the men who'd made this desperate stand. I wasn't sure exactly what had happened when Sark had taken the cube containing the ancient demon. I'd been brained from behind only moments before it had happened, so my recollection was unsteady. More than what I saw, I remembered feeling multiple wills being bound together even as they tore and twisted from each other. I feared the worst, but voicing only ill-bodings seemed less than helpful. The soldiers were on alert, that would have to be enough.

Stewart signalled the point team inside while the rest took up defensive positions, some facing in, some facing out. I hunkered in a rocky alcove next to Hadlynne, whose main attribute besides a hefty crop of dark freckles, was his determination to be supremely laconic. The man wouldn't use two words when one would do, and if he could get away with none, all the better.

I ground my teeth as the point team swept the deeper points of the compound. Waiting there in the stale, refuse-sodden air was agonising enough, but fearing at any moment the world might explode into bloody violence was nearly unbearable. My senses straining, I could only hear the occasional rustle of a nearby team member or the tread of those moving in the rooms beyond.

"Initial entry cleared."

I flinched as the words came through my earpiece.

"Central, proceed," Stewart growled. "Rear-guard, hold."

Hadlynne and I were just about to move from our position to join the central group when there was a snarled curse over the headset and a burst of weapons fire within the vault-like chamber.

"Contact!" a voice bellowed, and a high pitched shriek tore through the air. The subhuman sound set my teeth on edge and my skin prickled up into gooseflesh.

Half-formed visions of what new horror waited on the other side of the door materialized in my imagination, but as quickly as the shooting and screaming had started, it stopped.

"Bordeaux?" Stewart demanded in a low, rumbling voice.

There were a few more curses, these muttered, and then what sounded like someone sobbing.

"Clear, Sarge," Bordeaux reported, and then with obvious irritation added, "we've got a non-hostile survivor."

You could feel the exasperation in Stewart's tone as his commands went out again.

"Central, resume. Rear-guard, hold."

Passing through the rent portal, disgust rippled through me at the oily skein of the demon's psychic residue. I made sure to steer clear of the edges, not simply for their sharpness, but so that I wouldn't touch the filth that threatened to overwhelm my metallic sense.

Inside this central chamber was a long rectangle whose sides sported multiple doors to other passages. The far wall was a massive sheet of smoked glass or tinted plastic. The stuttering light made it glisten like a wall of seething black ice. Standing a few feet from this peculiar wall was Bordeaux's point team. Most had taken positions to cover the room's many points of access, but the fireteam leader stood with another soldier, rifles across the chests, looking down at a ragged form pawing at their feet. The blubbering noises were from the wretched creature on the floor.

Central fireteam moved to take positions in support of the point team, but taking a little initiative, I moved to the back toward the survivor. Hadlynne followed.

"Please ... please, before it comes back," he whined in a wheedling voice. A Brit by the sound of it. His clothes weren't just mussed and torn, but filthy.

"Care to explain what all the shooting was about?" Stewart asked as he faced his men, ignoring the wretch mewling at their feet.

"He attacked me," the other soldier offered with a shrug. A specialist who I thought was named Dalal or Dalel or something.

"He *hugged* you," Bordeaux corrected, his voice flat.

"Same difference," Dalal shrugged again. "Especially with him smelling like that."

"I'm sorry, s-s-so sorry," the man panted, pawing at the men's boots. "I was j-just so happy to see you. I've been hiding for days and d-days."

The man had begun to tremble, his frame shivering inside his ruined suit. He'd left off pawing at the soldier's feet, much to Dalal's relief, and wrapped his arms around himself. He began to rock on his knees, bending his head to bite down on the arm of his stained coat. Even through the fabric, I could hear a pitiful whine sliding between his clenched teeth.

"He was in the room?" Stewart asked, looking at the man for the first time.

"No, he came through there," Bordeaux answered, nodding to the last door on the left-hand wall before the smoked glass. "Dalal was securing it when he opened the door and hugged him."

Dalal bent his head and sniffed his sleeve, his nose wrinkling in disgust.

"If you smelled like this," he huffed, nodding down toward his offending arm, "then you'd call it an attack too."

Despite the thrumming tension, or perhaps because of it, I had to stifle a snort. As Bordeaux and Stewart turned to look at me, I realised I'd made a fatal error. Neither of them seemed to appreciate the humour of the situation.

"Something you'd like to add, Ms Bashir?" Stewart asked, clearly nonplussed.

I should have shrunk back with my tail between my legs, but I ignored the sergeant's question to crouch next to the man on the floor. The smell made my eyes water, but I gave him a gentle smile and spoke to him in a low, soothing tone.

"It's okay you're going to be safe now. We're here to bring you back home."

The whining noise stopped, but he continued to rock, his eyes darting to my face every so often, when he wasn't looking at the men with guns standing over him. I inched closer, feeling my skin wanting to jump up and run away, but keeping the same tender look by sheer willpower.

"You said you've been in here for days," I said. "Why didn't you leave?"

His eyes snapped toward the ravaged door, and a parched tongue rasped over his cracked lips.

"I was afraid," he whispered. "Afraid it would come back."

I nodded, wondering if the horror this man had endured had broken his mind. Even I, who possessed a way to fight the demon, had found Kezsarak terrifying. To a person helpless before his fury, I could only imagine the terror.

"The thing that did this," I asked, gesturing to the room, "did it kill everyone else? Everyone in the compound, I mean?"

Part of me fostered a spark of hope that Kezsarak had killed the awakened Ninurta. It might make Kezsarak even more terrifying, but I'd beaten him once before. He was a devil I knew.

"Everyone that fought him, yes," he sobbed, but sent a guilty glance at the corpses lying around us. "And then he went after the survivors from the escape tunnels."

"Escape tunnels?" Stewart barked, stepping closer. "We have no intel on escape tunnels."

The small man shied away from Stewart's gruff interjection, scooting closer to me. Our survivor's gaze darted between me and the sergeant, his preference clear in his alternatively cringing and pleading expression.

Stewart looked meaningfully toward me and nodded.

"Where are those escape tunnels?" I asked delicately, keeping my encouraging smile fixed.

"You can't get out that way!" he declared with a shrill cry. "He rigged them to collapse. They're blocked now, full of dead bodies."

He shuddered, and his hands shot up.

Instinct wouldn't be denied anymore, and I lurched backward to my feet, fearing an "attack" like Dalal had experienced. To my relieved surprise, his grimy hands didn't reach for me but clutched his head. He alternated between tugging on his limp, hair plastered scalp, and boring into his ears with grubby fingers.

"He laughed while he killed them!" he wailed. "I heard the big voice laughing over and over again while the other two argued. Even in the lowest maintenance shafts, I could hear it."

I stared at him, trying to figure out exactly what I'd just heard. The big voice? That had to be Kezsarak, but the others? And they were arguing?

Stewart leaned over and growled into my ear.

"We need to know about those escape tunnels, now."

I nodded and asked the man, "The other voices, what did they sound like?"

The survivor stopped scrabbling at his head and stared at me, and I wondered if he'd heard me clearly between his spasming attacks on his ears. The wretched little man began to bob his head, slowly at first, but with growing speed and ferocity.

"Yes-yes-yes-yes," he gibbered. "Two other voices besides the big one. Three! Three voices. I heard them before, when he saw me and then again when he went to the escape tunnels."

He pointed to a door on the wall opposite the one he'd come through.

"Even down that tunnel I could hear all three of them. Two argued with each other while the big one laughed as everyone died."

Stewart began to bark out directions for the point team to investigate. I crouched down again next to to the man, trying to hold his attention as soldiers moved around us.

"The other two voices," I pressed. "What did they sound like?"

His eyes followed the first members of the point team toward the door, and he began to shake his head vigorously.

"Can't get out that way. You can't!"

"Look at ME!" I snapped my fingers. His gaze ripped toward me, his expression wary.

"Tell me about the other voices."

His lip trembled, looking for all the world like an oversized child caught playing with matches.

"One was hard, sharp ... sounded angry, but also a little scared. It was telling the other voice to shut-up so it could do what had to be done."

It sounded like Sark. The end justifies the means; that was gospel to the self-serving traitor.

"And the other?" I urged.

He scratched his face. "It sounded almost um ... tired, kind of old. Maybe like a grandfather. It was that voice that saved me when he spotted me."

"Saved you?" I asked.

"I was trapped," he moaned and began wringing his hands. "He'd trapped me even as he killed everyone else in here. Then, when he was about to kill me, the old voice told me to run and set me free."

He clutched his legs and resumed rocking.

"I ran and hid."

My heart gave a painful thud at the evidence given supporting what I had feared. Lowe. My ghostly mentor and friend had been caught in a kind of dual possession with Kezsarak in Sark's body. Lowe's strong soul vying with Sark and Kezsarak for control in a perpetual struggle.

Despite the horror of Lowe's position, I couldn't help feeling some relief. Lowe wasn't gone, and unwittingly or not, he'd saved a messenger to pass that information along.

"Tunnel's blocked, like he said," Bordeaux reported over the wire. "Mess of casualties too."

"Acknowledged," Stewart grunted, and then he was at my shoulder.

"Ask about Ninurta, and then we'll get out of here," the sergeant commanded.

My mind still buzzing with the news about Lowe, the command jarred me back to the present.

"Was Ninurta here when he attacked?" I asked the survivor.

A dramatic and chilly change swept over the little man at the mention of Ninurta's name. The terror which had shone in his bulging, bloodshot eyes began to bleed away, and something like adoration or even longing took its place. The transformation was out of place yet so complete that an uncanny sense of wrongness crept up my spine.

"You know of the god-king?"

"Yes," I managed to force out. "Was he here during the attack?"

"Of course not," he cried, looking at me as though I'd suggested it was raining fish and chips outside. "If the bright and glorious one, the untarnished king, had been here, things would have been different ... very different."

The utter conviction, fanatical as the gleam of the dying woman in Fes, had me hiding another shiver. "Where is he then? Where is Ninurta?"

"He left, flew from here to carry the great news of his return. He stayed here only a few days to learn of the changed world and to learn some of our languages. Who but a god could learn so much so fast?"

Stewart and I shared an unsure glance.

"He is on his great mission, his great quest. Soon his wayward children will be gathered to him, and then they, under his guidance, will make the world anew. Upon the bones of the old world, will his kingdom rise, but he must have his children first. With them it will be a rule that has no end!"

Stewart gave a singularly dismissive grunt behind me, but I couldn't shake the sense of dread that crept over me when I heard those apocalyptic words. Gather his children? Did that mean the Inconquo? Make the world anew? What did that entail?

"Sarge," a voice hissed through the headset. "We've got movement back here."

"Copy, what are we—"

Stewart's words were drowned out by the roar of "Contact!" over the line and the sound of gunfire ripping out from the rear-guard.

The survivor screamed, high and frantic as he threw himself down, arms raised over his head.

"He's back!"

# SIX

Gunfire hammered out a furious staccato tempo, both from the rear-guard and some unseen foe in the chamber beyond. Most of the incoming fire deflected off the vault doors, but enough of the shots came whining through the opening that everyone in the room ducked and scrambled for cover.

Hadlynne hauled me by my shoulder behind an overturned steel table.

"Stay down, mum," my guardian barked as he dared a peek over the top of the table.

I pushed back the irritation at being directed to stay out of the fight, instead I focused my whole attention on my metallic sense, pushing through the bonded Rings and outward. I could hear Stewart issuing orders over the head-set, recalling the point team, I think, but it was just another distraction, so I popped the earpiece out.

When I first heard the call for contact and the survivor's panicked declaration, I'd been momentarily convinced that possessed Sark or even Ninurta had returned. My body clenched in terrified preparation for a supernatural onslaught, but as the rear-guard traded fire with an unseen enemy, I realised that didn't seem to be the case. Even if Sark or Ninurta had brought gun-toting cronies, they wouldn't waste their shots on the vault doors when they could simply rip them open.

No, at least for now, these seemed to all be ordinary men, however well trained, using ordinary weapons of war. *Metal* weapons of war.

A smile broke over my face.

That smile was quickly paired with sweat because it was a strain from the rear of the chamber to sense anything that far away. Thankfully with so much metal, from combat rifles, ammunition, and body armour, I could drag out a clearer picture of at least six enemy combatants.

I pegged their presence but I needed to get closer.

"I'm moving up," I shouted to Hadlynne as stray shots zipped around our cover like hellish wasps.

"What?" Hadlynne asked, but I was already in motion.

With an outstretched hand, I drew the steel table up with me as I rose, shaping it into a domed shield with a diameter my full height. Stepping over broken bodies, I moved toward the entrance, wincing a little less each time a shot glanced off the infused steel.

I was halfway to the entrance when Stewart's voice roared over the chug and chatter of gunfire.

"Bashir, get down, damn your eyes!"

He was crouching in a doorway, nursing a wound in his arm that had soaked his sleeve in blood. His face was pale and drawn with pain, but his expression was a mask of outright rage.

"Trust me," I shouted back, resuming my advance.

He looked about to give me a profanity-laden piece of his mind, but another shot sparked off his doorway, and I'd already moved too close to the rear-guard to hear him. The thunder of their combat rifles filled my ears, and the flash of their muzzle flares was enough to dazzle in the unsteady light.

I didn't bother with my typical sense, though, instead drawing my powers up behind my fabricated shield.

The six I'd pegged were the first to see my presence on the battlefield. Gun barrels twisted like snakes to join with trauma plates on chests, rendering their weapons useless while impeding their owners' movements.

The amount of enemy fire decreased, and I had a few seconds to feel proud of myself. I stretched my metallic senses outward, thinking to handle the next batch of hostiles the same way and realised with a start that the enemy had us vastly outnumbered. The six I'd first latched on to were only part of the vanguard.

We had them bottlenecked here, but even with me assisting, they were about to come pouring into the chamber beyond, and by sheer numbers we'd have a hard time keeping them out. We needed to find an alternative exit, fast, or this would turn into a bloodbath.

"Grenade!" someone screamed.

A trio of silver-grey spheres spun down into our midst.

On instinct, I threw two of them back with my powers, where they'd detonate among the confused enemy. The third bounced off the opening in the vault door and landed between two soldiers.

Slamming into action so hard and fast that my eyes blurred with tears, I inverted my shield and clamped it over the grenade. The explosive went off and would have blown the shield into a cloud of shrapnel if not for my powers bearing down. Instead, the wave's force rebounded between the floor and the straining particles of the shield. Distantly, the other grenades exploded, but I was barely aware of them as I focused on containing the blast in our midst.

By the time I let go with a gasp, the shield crumbled into glowing slivers of metal.

My head throbbed with the effort and my hands trembled as I looked around at our team. Crouched in protective postures and hidden behind what barriers they could find, but alive. The same could not be said of the attackers. Blinking around, my ears ringing, I saw the evidence of the other explosions from the enemies quarters... blood, smoke, and dust drifting through the churned air. More importantly, no one was shooting at us.

A quick sweep told me that the tunnels beyond were still full of enemies, but it seemed they weren't keen to rush in.

The grenades had bought us seconds that should not be wasted.

"Step back!" I shouted as I threw both of my hands out to the layers of metal composing the ruined vault door. "Stand clear of the door."

I wasn't sure if it was the fact that I'd just saved their lives or something in my voice that made them listen, but every member of the rear-guard scuttled backward.

The violence done to the huge door was incredible, something which only Kezsarak could have managed. For all that, though, there was still a lot of metal lying around, and though it wouldn't be like it was before, I could force enough of it back into shape to seal us off from the front half of the compound.

I threw my powers against the huge twisted spurs and peeling sheets of steel, iron, and titanium. A heavy groan issued from the metal and squeals of protest rose like a shrieking chorus. The sheer quantity of material I was moving made my limbs tremble as I bore down on the cantankerous auras. They gave way one after the other with gathering momentum.

Voices raised, some in alarm, some in awe, but I couldn't spare the effort to decipher what they were saying. The pressure of the energy I poured into the vault door throbbed through my skull, my teeth grinding so hard I hoped they wouldn't crack. It was almost there, the pieces being forced into alignment even as I drove spikes of focus, prepping sections to be welded together. A rush of heat stung my skin, and my legs began to buckle. I threw every last ounce of mental energy I could scrape for one last push as I fell onto my knees.

Half a dozen hisses rose and then were snuffed out as a great crash sounded from the door like a resounding gong.

My eyelids felt like they were weighted with lead, but I managed to drag them up enough to see the sealed portal. It was a mashed, Frankensteinian thing and not nearly as sound as it had once been, but it was solid, and the enemy would at least have to take the time to set explosives.

As if in impotent protest, the sharp klink of small arms fire deflected off the sealed door. Shakily, I climbed to my feet.

"What the bloody hell do you think you're doing?"

Stewart advanced on me, his wounded arm dangling a bandage and medical tape. The team medic, a fellow named Ramid, trailed after him, his normally genial features set into a smouldering scowl. He was juggling scissors and bandages from an open medpac.

"I sealed the entrance," I said dumbly, keeping my eyes from wandering to the rest of the team for support. I'd taken the initiative, I couldn't ask any of them to defend me.

"And sealed us in a damned tomb, you stupid bint!" Stewart roared as he reached me, his good arm raised with a clenched fist. I thought he was going to take a swing at me, but Ramid snatched his wounded arm and hauled him backward.

"Bastard!" Stewart bellowed and made an awkward cross-body swipe at Ramid, who hardly had to lean back to let it pass him. For his part, the medic seemed too preoccupied with finishing the bandage on Stewart's arm to notice the sergeant's fury.

"Hold still, Sarge," Ramid instructed in a no-nonsense tone as he set to work. "If we don't get this patched, you'll be too busy bleeding out to bawl anyone out."

A stream of caustic invective was Stewart's only reply as he held still and let himself be tended to. As the tap of verbal acid trickled off, Stewart squeezed his eyes closed for a second, took a deep breath, and craned his head to look at me. The rest of him started to follow, but a tug and sharp words from Ramid held him in place.

"Ignoring that you've trapped us in here without even checking with your superior," Stewart said through clenched teeth, "do you have a plan to go with your ... rash actions, *Ms Bashir*."

I couldn't keep from wincing a little at the way he said my name, but I squared my shoulders as I met his frosty glare.

"My ability to sense metal told me that we were about to be overrun," I began hoping that my voice was pitched loud enough for everyone to hear. "They were in arms and had numbers that would have overrun us very quickly once they mobil—"

"You mean in your completely inexperienced, utterly untrained opinion," Stewart interjected. "That's how ya ken this situation. As a civilian."

"Even a civilian can tell that being outnumbered five to one by an enemy armoured to the teeth is a good way to lose," I snapped back, appreciating the slightest shift in the stance of the men around me. "And those were just the ones I was aware of in the tunnels. There may have been more beyond them that I couldn't sense."

Stewart stared at me for a long moment as Ramid finished his bandaging and then looked at the sealed doorway. The sounds of gunfire ricocheting off had ceased, and only the faintest muffle could be heard from the other side, but the distinct impression of orders being issued and bodies moving was present.

"Alright," Stewart sighed, head shaking, suddenly looking two decades older. "You're a big damn hero for buying us minutes, instead of one blaze of glory. We still have no way out."

"The escape tunnels," I said and then looked around for the survivor. He stood in front of the far wall, hands splayed across the dark surface. "He can tell us where they lead."

Stewart looked at the shivering little man and then swung his gaze to Bordeaux, who had led point team back when the shooting started. Bordeaux shook his head once, his expression as flat and unreadable as ever.

"Remember the part where the tunnels are collapsed?" Stewart asked, tired eyes waiting for another disappointing response.

"I can open them," I promised, ignoring the weak feeling in my limbs from the energy I'd already used. I squared my shoulders and put my hands behind my back in a confident stance. It wouldn't do any good for the soldiers to see my hands shake.

Stewart looked at the sealed door, then at Bordeaux, who stared back. Stewart finally shook his head and then met my gaze.

"I hope so, lass," he sighed with a shrug and a wince, putting his hand on his injured arm, a gesture I thought was unconscious. "Otherwise, you just bought us enough time to think about how inevitable our deaths are."

With that, he raised his voice to address the rest of the security team.

"All right, you lot, we've got minutes before they blow that door down."

As if on cue, a thunderclap sounded on the other side of the door, that left our ears ringing. The portal trembled but didn't give way. As the ringing subsided, there were more shouted commands and the sound of hurried movement.

"Point's going to clear out what they can for Ms Bashir while Central does the fastest sweep for intel we've ever done. Rear-guard keeps our arses covered."

"As usual," someone muttered, and a few forced laughs followed.

"You know your business," Stewart called out. "Hop to!"

As the soldiers rushed to their duties, I nodded toward the survivor, and with Stewart just behind me, we approached. He didn't notice us, his face pressed against the thick, tinted material, fingers tracing over two spiderwebbed sections where stray shots had struck.

"Hey," I said, realising that we'd made it this far without the man's name. "You never told us your name."

I was halfway through repeating the question when he began to speak, his voice low and choked.

"I watched him born anew," he said, eyes fixed ahead as his forehead rested on the darkened glass. "Saw it with my own eyes. Saw it right there."

My skin rippled up into goose bumps. But though my stomach felt like a cold lump, I moved closer and looked through the shaded wall.

The lights had been fitful throughout the compound, but in that room, through the dark glass, was the steady glow of work lamps shining over a bowl dug into the stone. Within the bowl in concentric rings expanding out from a cavity at the exact centre, jagged crests of metal stabbed upward. It was like a detonation at the centre of a pool of molten metal which had sent up sharp waves, only for the metal to cool and harden at the instant of its violent expulsion. It was a cold, bladed court arrayed around a single point where something momentous happened, now left as an eternal, silent testament.

"What was it like?" I was unable to tear my eyes away.

He drew in a breath that was equal parts pain and longing.

"Like dying," he whispered. "At first, it was terror, then acceptance as the inevitable stole over me. Then it was freedom."

He turned, eyes boring into me.

"I was his then. We all were. Even my superior, Herr Niemand, threw himself at his feet. Before his naked feet, we all worshipped. Just as you will soon worship."

I dragged my eyes from the alien nursery of Ninurta's rebirth, an argument nearly coming to my tongue until I saw his face. Adoring tears rolled down his cheeks, and for a bare second, I thought they were for the memory he'd shared, but then I saw the way he was looking at me. The emotional display was for me, as he looked at me with rapt attention and wonder.

"You are one of his children." He smiled and drew his hands from the wall to clasp them in front of him in reverence. "You will help him bring about the new order, the remaking of the world."

I recoiled, ready to tell him that I'd never be a servant of such evil. But arguing with a brainwashed zealot wouldn't help anyone and I could feel Stewart growing restless behind me.

"Well I can't do anything if I am trapped down here," I retorted. "I think I can open the escape tunnels, but I need to know where they go. Can you tell us?"

His compliant demeanour clouded over with confusion, and he looked from me to Stewart and back.

"Didn't they provide you with a layout when they sent you on the rescue?"

I froze as a realization struck. He thought we were *with* the Group of Winterthür. A look of understanding flashed between Stewart and I like lightning. Why had we not realized it before? One wrong word could turn this man from a resource into a liability.

"The briefing was incomplete due to interdepartmental conflict," Stewart offered, sparing me from having to come up with a fumbling explanation. "Herr Niemand's branch could not render timely assistance, so we were scrambled from Frau Nichts' branch, but for security reasons were not given complete layouts upon the contingency that this was a false alarm."

This seemed to be more than enough for our survivor, as he was nodding before Stewart had even finished. I couldn't help but be impressed at our leader's quick thinking and smooth delivery. The Sarge was an impressive liar.

"Of course, of course," the little man muttered. "The tunnels come out along the northern ridgeline above the valley floor. At least I think so."

I turned to Stewart.

"Can we have the helicopters pick us up there?"

Stewart looked grim.

"We'll need to get closer to the surface," he said with a grunt. "And hope that we aren't out of range."

---

"ALMOST THERE," I murmured as I shifted more rubble upward with a tongue of metal that had once been a structural girder.

A hand curled into a rictus claw jutted from the splintered rock for an instant before being entombed once more. I'd lost track of the corpses or pieces of corpses I'd seen. The tunnels were nearly choked with civilian operatives and technicians, and as I shoved load after load of pulverised rock, it seemed there was no end to the carnage.

"Almost there," I grunted again, driving another spike of power through the Rings and out, clearing another short stretch before shuffling forward. My clothes were soaked with perspiration, and even my boots were damp with the stuff. I stood there for a second, my hands on my knees, dragging a breath in before surrendering it with a reluctant wheeze. Not for the first time, I wondered if there was enough air down here to sustain all of us, but dwelling on the thought didn't make things any easier.

"Bashir, water."

I looked up in time to catch the canteen tossed my way by Ramid, and without a word, gulped a few mouthfuls.

My camel-hump, a backpack born sack of water complete with a handy straw, had been drained quickly, and now the rest of the team was passing canteens up to me. The stifling air combined with the effort was sucking the moisture out of my body and onto my skin, but thanks to their efforts, I hadn't collapsed into mummification just yet.

"Almost there," I gasped and slammed back another big swallow of water before tossing the canteen back and pushing forward.

The tunnel was dark except for the flashlights of the security team, beams strobing forward and backward, but I didn't need the light. For the moment, my world was reduced to what my metal sense could tell me about the remaining structure of the tunnel and what I could move where. I wormed my way through, the head of a line of soldiers. Strained minutes seemed like hours, as I fear the moment of a call from rear-guard that we'd been found. I'd heard two more explosions, but so far no call of a breach.

I pushed and scraped, shoved and shuffled the rubble over and over again, bracing the tunnel with reshaped spans of metal as I went. Beads of sweat poured down the sides of my face as I bent or fused as needed, ensuring the walls were as stable as I could make them. No sense in clearing a section just to have it collapse as the team came through behind me.

Another flurry of clearings later, and the air in the tunnel changed. At first, it was just a welcome coolness on my cheek, then it seemed less choked with decomposition and dust. I could sense the surface nearing and my heartbeat surged with hope, my energy renewed.

Stewart rasped somewhere behind me in the marching procession of lights. "Jameson, see if you can raise the birds over the comm-sat."

In a burst of excited power, I cleared out another section as Jameson sought to arrange our rendezvous with aerial rescue. More rock scraped and rumbled, and I pushed forward and set to work again before realising I needed to pace myself or I'd black out before we reached our destination. Hope and adrenalin could only do so much.

I grinned in the dark despite the bone-deep fatigue, sending my metallic sense to stretch to its utmost hoping for the telltale auras. Sure enough, I felt the resonance of a section where the tunnel was still whole, less than a dozen metres through the rubble. Beyond this, I could sense the change in metal as the tunnel became a bar-grated portal to the surface, complete with rail-flanked steps.

A sound that was part laugh, part sob wracked my body but died off as the last of my metallic sense trailed along the periphery by the door and felt something familiar. The complex metallurgy of combat rifles, the sturdy steel of trauma plates.

The enemy was waiting for us on the other side.

"Sergeant Stewart," I called behind me, and there was a rattling and grunting as he came to join me.

"What?" Stewart snarled around the small flashlight clenched in his mouth like a cigar.

"We are only ten metres from the way out," I said, trying to force my tone to be even despite the exhaustion and anxiety plaguing my breathing. "But we have a problem."

He gave an impatient jerk of his chin. *Well?*

"They've got men outside the tunnel exit," I explained. "Once we go through, we'll probably have seconds before they hear us and clog the way out with gunfire."

The light bobbed as Stewart nodded, taking it in stride. His calm demeanour bolstered my weary spirit. I felt ready to cry, but if our leader felt as unruffled as he looked by my discovery, then surely there was hope.

"We're going to have to punch our way out."

"Yes," I sighed and then through the haze felt an idea bludgeon its way to the fore.

"If you can have the whole team ready to move on my go," I began mustering myself to the plan even as I spoke it, "I can use the last bit of rubble as a smokescreen to drive out the tunnel exit as I shove the grate away. If they follow the dust cloud out, they can make a way through."

Stewart considered this then flicked his chin up at me, the flashlight dazzled me momentarily.

"What about you?" he asked with a grunt.

I looked back down the wormhole I'd carved.

"I need to collapse the tunnel so they can't follow us."

Stewart gave something like a snort, and when he spoke, I swore I could hear mirth in his voice.

"Dinna worry aboot that," he told me, his brogue extra thick. "Had to find a use fer those noot-crackers after all."

I just grasped his meaning when somewhere below us a tectonic rumble shook the dust from the walls, followed by a grinding crash.

"Breach," came the static laden report of the rear-guard.

Stewart and I stared at each other in the dark, and then he gave me a hard but jovial slap across the back.

"Do what you got to lass," Stewart growled, a wet, hungry sound. "We've got yer six."

I didn't have time to bask in the rush of heady accomplishment to be treated so by the crusty sergeant. Straightening, I tucked it away for future reflection and turned back to the rubble clogged tunnel.

"Almost there," I snarled in my own leonine tone and then launched my powers forward.

# SEVEN

"Herr Niemand, eh?" Marks asked, her voice dancing between the edges of amused and concerned.

I wasn't sure if the question was directed at me – had I mentioned Herr Niemand? – but I was in no mood to answer Marks' probings.

The office chair I was sitting in was unusually comfortable and gave only the slightest creak as I settled deeper. After our daring escape from the tunnels in Iraq, I'd done nothing but sleep between zombie-like shuffling from helicopter to plane to van, but it wasn't enough. I was tired.

"Yes, mum," Stewart said. "Half of what the wretch said was loony whingin' but that much was clear."

My thoughts wandered to the things the pitiful man had said concerning my connection to Ninurta. My mind swam with half-formed images, huge and ancient buildings, thrones wet with blood, and the sound of cities dying as mountains crumbled. Behind these horrific vistas was a burning awareness that some vast intelligence drove them all, racing forward. What forward meant I wasn't sure exactly, but I was certain of some insidious purpose the same way you know you aren't alone in a room.

*Ibukun*

The whisper was soft as silk, but I felt its pull like gravity.

*Ibby*

I knew I needed to fight, to shove it away, but I was exhausted body and soul.

*Ibukun Bashir*

The will behind the whisper slowly enfolded me like a velvet-lined python coiling around my mind.

"Ibukun Bashir! Attention!"

The martial bark, suffused with years of assumed command, smashed through the encircling glamour, and I started awake.

Sitting bolt upright, my seat tilted and I tumbled forward. It was then, in that half-second of falling, that I realised my chair hadn't been on the floor. I landed hard on my shoulder with a wounded *uffh* and rolled to my back. Suspended above me--spinning in a slow orbit--was my office chair, a second chair, and several office items.

I hadn't felt the current of power keeping the objects suspended like that, and the very second I realised it, the floating items did too. I scuttle-scooted on my back and posterior just in time. The chairs crashed down together, one losing an arm in the fall, while the hole-punch, stapler, and paper clips pattered and thumped down like hailstones.

Hoisting myself up onto my elbows, I looked around. I was still in Marks' office. Stewart and Marks were standing by the door, the sergeant standing protectively in front of his superior despite one arm bound to his chest by a harnessed sling.

"What happened?' I gaped. "Is everyone alright?"

"You tell us," Stewart said, his voice flat and hard to match his gaze.

I flushed and had a childish urge to jump up and run away. This wasn't the first time my powers had been at work while I slept, but it was the first time anyone else had been around when it happened.

"I ... I'm not sure." I climbed to my feet. "I must have fallen asleep. Sorry."

I bent down to right the chairs and gather the scattered office detritus.

"Sorry," I muttered again as I put the arm of the office chair on the seat. "I'm not sure what happened."

I wasn't sure if seeing me picking up after myself like a repentant child had helped, or just the fact that no one seemed to be under attack, but Stewart and Marks both moved back into the room. Marks took her seat, a venerable and immaculate piece of leather and dark wood that hadn't answered my metallic summons. Thankfully, her computer seemed to be mounted to her desk, though she took some care in setting everything else back in its proper place. Stewart remained standing, his expression one of acute attention. I finished making a little pile of office bits n' bobs on the corner of Marks' desk, squirming under her scrutiny.

"Thank you, Ibby," she said with practiced civility as I stepped back and stood next to the broken chair, hands folded in front of me.

"Again, I'm sorry," I offered and my cheeks flushed again.

Marks gave me a long look, and then one of her expert smiles appeared, bidding me to be at ease.

"Not at all, my dear, happens all the time," she said, pointedly ignoring the quick look Stewart gave her. "But I do think you need to be checked out to make sure everything is alright."

I shifted from one foot to the other, trying to find the right thing to say.

"I don't think it is a ... eh, physical issue, ma'am," I said suddenly finding it hard to look her in the eye. "I think it's more ..."

I searched for the word and remembered with a pang how Lowe would have described such things.

"More of a metaphysical issue."

Marks nodded, and her eyes crinkled at the corners.

"Good thing I keep a metaphysician on staff, then."

---

"I THINK Ms Marks was being a little ... dramatic in her description," Dr Hiroki Emoto explained as we sat drinking tea in his office. "I function more as an assessor than a counsellor, though I am a very good listener if that helps."

The small, not-quite-smile that followed was equal parts self-deprecation and invitation, and I couldn't help finding the slight man endearing. I was glad for this as when I'd first stepped into his office I'd been a wreck of nerves and suspicion.

His office was an exercise in minimalism, except for a few curated plants and a single large photograph hanging on the wall. The picture looked like golden sand dunes rising out of white rock, with a dark churning sea on the horizon, all lit by a harsh dawn or grim sunset. The landscape, sinister and alien in its strange, inhuman proportions, made me even more nervous than I'd been when Marks had first told me I was to see a metaphysician.

I couldn't help feeling that the bare, sterile aesthetic was because this was where they would be strapping me down to do invasive tests. The spartan decor was just to make sure nothing got in the way of my examination.

Yet, no scalpel and probe armed legions had assailed me, only a thin Japanese man who'd offered me a seat and then some tea with gentle civility.

"Is there something you would like to talk about?" he prompted, bringing me back to the moment.

There was, but as nice as he seemed, I wasn't sure Dr Emoto was the person I wanted to talk with. The two people who I'd usually go to with such things were currently indisposed: one in a coma, the other fused to a treacherous enemy. Even Uncle Iry, bless him, was still recovering and didn't need any extra burdens.

Though his expression had remained patient and his tea-sipping frightfully quiet, I felt the doctor's eyes on me.

"That picture," I nodded toward a photograph on the wall. "I don't recognise the desert. Is it Africa? The Middle East?"

Dr Emoto looked at me over his cup of tea for a long second before giving his head the slightest shake.

"No," he answered, eyes never leaving me. "It is actually not a desert at all. It is a stretch of sand dunes outside the village of Higashidōri, where my father was born. The dunes are used almost exclusively by the Ministry of Defence, but many years ago, I was given the opportunity to assist them and had the good fortune to take that picture after a fresh snowfall."

I squinted and realised what I'd taken to be a foundation of white rock was actually drifted blankets of snow. The realisation made the photograph seem a little less sinister, if not any less alien.

"You don't keep much in your office," I observed, to which the doctor nodded and gave a small smile. "So why that picture?"

Dr Emoto's eyebrows rose incrementally, then he set his teacup down.

"I am happy to answer this question," he said, somehow driving utter sincerity into every word. "But may I ask that after I do, you answer a question for me?"

I gave the slight man a once over, a hundred and one different suspicions running through my mind before I gave a stiff nod of assent. I supposed if I didn't like what he was asking, I could not answer or lie. I wouldn't feel good about either and was terrible at the latter, but I supposed this was part of the whole dance; give and take.

"I keep a copy of this photograph in all my offices," he said, turning to look at the dunes. "Because it reminds me of that wonderful moment of beholding. As a young boy visiting relatives in the village, I was never allowed to go near the dunes. They filled me with a curious longing, and though I hardly spoke of it, the desire to see them, especially in the snow, never left me. Then through no intention of my own, I was there, seeing what as a child had been a fantasy. It was beautiful, terrible, and humbling, standing there shivering before what felt like a gate to an impossible world."

He turned back to me, his dark eyes glistening.

"It is the same thing I felt when I began to work for The Nakesh Corporation and witnessed my first paranormal event. I've borne witness over and over again to a world most can't imagine. I use this photograph to remind me of that, and to remind myself to be mindful and humble before that truth."

"That's ... an impressive answer," I admitted lamely, acutely aware that my turn to give an answer was coming. "How many offices do you have?"

"Altogether, three. This one here in London. Another in Sweden, and a field station in the wilds of North America which I'm not permitted to pinpoint." Taking up his tea, he gave me a quick wink. "But we have a bargain, and that was two questions I answered."

I let out a breath and crossed my arms over my chest. "Alright, let me have it. What's your question?"

Dr Emoto nodded again, took out a small notepad and pen with one hand, before setting the tea down.

"In reading the reports of the last mission, I noted that you took no direct action against the enemy combatants. You disabled their weapons or deflected their attacks, but I don't see any report of actively using your abilities to attack hostiles. Is this how your powers operate?"

"Not always," I said, remembering with a degree of uncomfortable pride the times I'd put down men twice my size with a thought. "There have been several times I've knocked men out cold. I also dropped a refinery on top of a demon once. Didn't work in the end, but it was one of my more aggressive uses of power."

Emoto nodded as he jotted notes on his pad. He looked up, his expression inscrutable.

"May I ask then, if you are capable of using your powers more aggressively, why not compel the metal to kill those who were attempting to kill you and the team? It would have been more final. No?"

I considered the question before recalling Uncle Iry's words stinging my ears: *You are no assassin, Ibby.*

"I suppose it's because killing people, even bad people, is not what I want to use my powers for," I shifted in my seat. "I guess it comes with being an Inconquo."

"Could you elaborate, please?" Emoto asked between further scribblings.

"When I found out I was an Inconquo from Professor Lowe, he told me that I was part of a long line of guardians. That resonated with me and still does. Using my powers takes its toll, but when I am using them to protect others, I find I have more to give even when I feel used up. I'd like to believe that's because of what it means to be Inconquo."

Emoto nodded and then looked up from his pad, and the smallest frown creased his features.

"Very interesting, and I thank you for being transparent," his eyes flicked down to his notes. "But would you allow me another question?"

"Sure."

"Thank you."

Emoto bobbed his head and smiled, but I could tell that there was a level of discomfort crinkling the corners of his eyes and making his smile brittle.

"Of primary concern is defeating the entity known as Ninurta, the progenitor of the Inconquo. Does the threat he poses in any way alter your perception or the application of your abilities as a member of his bloodline?"

My mouth opened, a sharp rebuttal halfway up my throat before I snapped my teeth together and choked the words back down. The question was a fair one, but the implications lifted my hackles.

"I ... I don't know." I retreated against the back of my chair.

Emoto studied me a moment longer and then was about to say something when there was a knock on the door. Emoto's brow furrowed, but before he could respond, the door opened. I turned to see Marcus at the door, his face flushed.

"Ibby," he gasped, pointing back down the hallway toward the elevator as he panted. "You need to come with me."

My gaze whipped to Emoto, who was doing an admirable job concealing his irritation at the intrusion. His attention shifted from Marcus to me, as if to say *your call.*

"Can it wait?" I asked Marcus. "Marks told me to meet with Dr Emoto, we're in the middle of things."

"Ibby," he growled, "you need to get up there now. It's Jackie!"

# EIGHT

She'd started breathing on her own shortly after I'd left and had woken up about an hour before I'd arrived back with the security team, but they'd neglected to let me know – on top of not letting Uncle Iry and Marcus know that I'd returned. Marcus had spied Stewart on the medical floor and realised I was back. His flushed and agitated appearance in Dr Emoto's office was the result of trying to find me.

We'd practically flown without touching the ground from Dr.Emoto's office to the elevator.

"How is she?" I forced aside my frustration at having not been told immediately to focus on Jackie.

"She's weak," he said leaning against the elevator wall. "They still have her on oxygen, and IV fluids. She's not in pain, but she fades in and out a bit from the medications."

I nodded, my heart pounding with relief among other things. Two days ago they weren't sure if she would ever wake up. This was a gift, a miracle.

"Ibby." Marcus lowered his voice.

"I'm fine," I insisted, assuming he was worried about me. I shook my head and straightened from the slumped lean I'd adopted. "Just tired, that's all."

"No." Marcus shook his head. "There's something else ..."

His tone caught my attention like a sharp hook, and I looked at him, eyes narrowing at his pained expression. A lurching, primitive sense ignited my nerves, forcing exhaustion to the back of my mind.

"What?" My voice was sharp and high, my throat closing painfully around the word.

"Jackie," he paused, "she can't feel anything below the middle of her back. The doctors don't know if it's a piece of the weapon still lodged in there or just the trauma, but ..."

His face fell as he watched the impact this had on me, unable to bear his burdensome news.

Cold flooded my gut and my breath hitched as my words tumbled from numb lips. I braced a hand against the elevator's wall as it lurched to a stop and the world seemed to spin.

"Jackie's paralysed."

---

WE WALKED to Jackie's room, determined to stay calm and in control. Closing my eyes for a brief moment, I took a breath before stepping inside.

Jackie reclined against pillows, her features swollen with fluids and ghostly pale. Uncle Iry was beside her, sitting in his wheelchair, his weathered skin hung around his gaunt face. His eyes were focused on her, and her hand was in his.

Neither noticed me as I hung there in the doorway, Marcus at my back, my body locked into place as I beheld the two dearest people in the world to me in their wounded grace.

They were smiling as they chatted; Jackie's brilliant smile undiminished by discoloured lips. But the smiles were haunted, ethereal things.

The truth stole around my neck like a strangling cord and kept me from moving – even breathing. It was me and all the trouble that had come with me which had left them wounded like this. How could this be worth it? How could all this pain be justified, especially visited on people who'd done nothing to deserve it?

The overwhelming urge to flee, to run and hide shivered through me. My rebellious limbs twitched fitfully, but I managed an unsteady lurch backward before a strong pair of arms braced me.

"In you go," Marcus whispered, his voice sad and unyielding. "You both need this."

The urge to flee melted, but Marcus had to guide me a few steps into the room.

Jackie's head turned. Her eyes widened. "Ibby?"

The voice was so paper-thin I wouldn't have recognised it as my darling, bubbly friend if I hadn't seen her mouth move. It was all I could do to look in those soft doe eyes, my tongue cleaving to the roof of my mouth.

Marcus let go of me but kept a hand on my back as I staggered a few steps closer. All I saw were IV and oxygen tubes: reminders of her inescapable infirmity, the cost of being my best friend. A lump grew in my throat.

"Oh come now, luv." She chuckled weakly, one unsteady arm reaching out. "I've looked worse."

I reached her on unsteady legs and took her cold fingers in mine. Gone was the strong, warm grip of the party girl who'd grown into a warrior woman. In its place was a limp collection of frail bones and wasted flesh wrapped in the thinnest of skin. I felt the trembling in her hand and knew the effort taxed her.

"I'm so sorry," I sobbed, hot tears racing down my cheeks. "I'm just so sorry."

Jackie looked up at me, confusion crinkling her smooth brow.

"What?" She studied my face through glazed eyes. "Why?"

My knees gave way as another sob tore its way out of my chest, and I knelt next to her bed. My forehead pressed against the mattress, the smells of rubbing alcohol and detergent assaulting my nose. I wanted to curl into myself with grief and pain, a brittle ball of misery.

"It's all my fault," I groaned, unable to look at her but keeping her frail hand clutched in mine. "I did this to you. I'm so sorry, Jackie."

Jackie tugged weakly to free her hand, and though my heart broke in two I released my hold. I couldn't blame her. The conviction of that thought beat more sobs out of me and I wept into the edge of the mattress: too ashamed to do anything useful, too broken to flee.

Then I felt shivering fingers cradle my head. "Ibby. Look at me."

I shook my head softly, but her hand stroked my hair until, through tear blurred eyes, I looked up into my best friend's face.

Her voice was a caress of gentle reproof. "You saved me. I would have died if you hadn't carried me out."

"But you wouldn't have been there in the first place if it weren't for me. It's my fault. *All* of this is my fault."

Jackie's smile spread like the dawn.

"Your fault that you answered the call in your blood to protect others? Your fault that you saved me from the worst of guys like you've always done? Your fault that you inspired me to be a better, stronger woman than I ever thought possible? You have to take credit for the good, too.

"I-I, oh, Jackie!" I rose and pressed myself into her weak but willing embrace. "I just want you to be okay."

Jackie's arms folded around me, and her fingers, light as breeze ran across my shoulders and the back of my head.

"I'm with you luv," she whispered softly. "That's halfway, isn't it?"

---

"Ibby."

I groaned and shifted in my sleep.

"Ibby, wake up."

The voice, masculine but soft, had a note of urgency that dug at my sleeping mind, demanding attention.

"What?" The word slurred into an irritated groan, as I refused to open my eyes.

"Ibby, you need to get up, now."

That urgency again, a little sharper this time.

Stifling a growl of frustration, I blinked the last murky mercies of sleep away. I'd fallen asleep in the chair next to Jackie's bed again. As I forced myself to focus, I saw Jackie sleeping soundly before me. If not for the even rise and fall of her chest, she might have been a wax figure in a museum exhibit. The familiar pangs of guilt threatened to distract me from the voice that had awoken me, but a large hand on my shoulder drew my attention.

"Ibby, you need to come."

I turned my head to see my uncle leaning forward in his wheelchair. A completely different guilt at my grouchiness snapped me into sharp wakefulness. I stood and followed Uncle Iry as he rolled himself to the door.

"Best 'it the bog," Hadlynne began as soon as I stepped into the hallway. He looked me up and down before giving a despairing shake of his head. "We're off."

His Yorkshire accent was hard enough to decipher, but with so little to work with, I was stumped. I looked at Uncle Iry for help, but he sat staring up at the man as though he were not sure what Hadlynne *was* much less what had been said.

"Come again?" I asked.

"Fresh 'teligence, fresh target, Yer a might bit bogeyed, eh? F'gured you'd be chuffed."

Now I understood why Hadlynne hardly ever talked: there was no point.

"Fresh ... what?"

"I heard the word target," Uncle Iry offered helpfully still studying the freckled soldier like he belonged in a lab somewhere.

"Bloody faffin' eejits." Hadlynne growled then crossed his arms and scowled at us so fiercely his freckles turned three shades darker.

"We've got a new target," I parrotted as the pieces fell into place. "We have a new target, and I need to get ready."

Uncle Iry nodded sagely, then squinted in studious inquiry at Hadlynne.

"Bah!" Hadlynne snarled and turned on his heels, lapsing into his natural silence as he stomped toward the elevator.

"Best follow him," Uncle Iry advised, adding "Marcus and I will keep her company. Don't worry. Jackie is in good hands." He squeezed my arm.

I swallowed the lump in the back of my throat and nodded. With a kiss on the top of Uncle Iry's head, I followed the fuming Yorkshireman.

# NINE

"Whose plan was this?" I growled as bullets peppered the stone wall I hunkered behind with Hadlynne. The dust and chips of stone sparkled in the Spanish sun.

Behind our position a steep slope – two degrees from a cliff – plunged to a beautiful Mediterranean shoreline some ten or fifteen metres below. If it hadn't been for the screams, curses, and discharging firearms, I would have described the little fishing hamlet south of Calpe as idyllic. True, the dilapidated fish cannery we'd come to "reconnoitre" was a sore spot with its peeling paint and industrial-grade stink, but the weather was mild, the surrounding mountains majestic, and the sea a brilliant blue.

As we approached, nearly a third of the industrial compound had erupted into a mass of splinters and shrapnel seconds before the shooting started. Stewart, to his credit, had barked orders almost immediately. While I was still pulling my jaw off the floor, point squad advanced along the opposite flank of the eruption while the central squad moved to secure the seemingly unmanned front entrance. Hadlynne had practically dragged me as the rear-guard moved to cover the ruins of the cannery that had been nearest the tightly wound road.

Shots rang out from the ruins when we tried to cross the road, and everyone had scrambled for cover.

Our mission had turned from reconnaissance with a potential raid, to a full-blown gun battle in mere seconds.

The profanity-laden reports to Stewart from team members suggested their return-fire wasn't having much success.

A shot skipped off the top of the wall above my head, and I cringed low enough for my breath to kick up the dust at my feet. I didn't want to stay here another second, vulnerable in a very poor position. And given the sour tang I'd sensed at detonation, I knew just who had done it.

My metallic senses strained. Like raking leaves I gathered every bit and bob of metal I could find, mostly shards and fragments from the explosion. I couldn't see them from where I crouched, but I heard them scrape and tinkle as they bounced off the road and each other. Shots from both sides slackened a little as the combatants gaped at the glittering dervish.

"Can someone give me a direction?" I asked into my headset through gritted teeth.

A brief pause, then "Two o'clock."

The dervish became a cyclone of metal shards. A terrified spasm of gunfire sliced harmlessly through the gathering storm, pattering across the stone.

"My turn," I whispered.

Men roared and wailed as the twisting, stinging fragments lashed over and through their position in the ruins. Curls of metal sheeting and slivers of fractured nails and bolts scourged the area like a swarm of locusts. I dared a look over the wall to see men springing up, covering their heads with both arms, and casting weapons aside as they ran. Glinting under the Mediterranean sun, the flecks of metal looked like enraged fireflies from hell.

Separated from their impromptu gun nests, the men appeared to be locals: leathery blokes who would have looked natural on a fishing boat or driving a flock over the rough hills. Some raced about in circles, not noticing they'd escaped the worst of my now dissipating storm. Others crept along on knees and elbows like strange penitents, not daring to look up from beneath their clasped hands. A few staggered forward clapping hands to thin gashes on their face and arms. Altogether there were more than a half dozen of them in the shattered stockyard.

"Sitting ducks," Bordeaux growled. Point and central had used my distraction to creep along the front of the building. There had been no clear shot into the cannery before, but now they had the enemy dead to rights.

"What's the plan, Sarge?" the corporal asked as I let the remaining scraps tumble to the ground.

Tension crackled in the air, and the world seemed to hold its breath. All the security team's weapons were trained on the stunned and defenceless men standing out in the open. Had our places been reversed, I doubted those men would have hesitated to kill us. The whole squad appeared to lean forward eagerly.

"I can secure them." I climbed over the wall intending to jog across the road to where Stewart squatted with the central squad.

"Bashir!" Stewart snarled, his voice low but forceful through my headset. "Get back to cover!"

"Give me a second." There'd be hell to pay for this later, but I cared more about avoiding further carnage than I did about Stewart's wrath.

I skirted around them, reaching out to a broad section of tin roof. It warbled as I lifted it off the ground, then gave a tortured screech as I tore its corrugations into strips. The men in the yard cringed and recoiled, their eyes bulging in fear. A few genuflected as their gazes wandered back to the rifle barrels levelled at them.

Stepping over the remnants of the stockyard's fence, one hand held out to shaping bonds, I met the eyes of the men I was trying to save.

"That's an order, lassie!" Stewart hissed.

I was sweating, but a chill clawed its way up my spine. I was defying direct orders, but I couldn't risk these men's lives. I moved to work faster, making as many strips as there were men.

Out of the corner of my eye, I saw Stewart rise. I had seconds before he either dragged me out of the way or told the team to open fire. With a less than gentle shove, I sent the strips of metal to loop around the chests and knees of the men in the yard. A few screamed as their legs were pinned together. A few flopped over, almost comically, their expressions dramatic enough for a Three Stooges film. But they were alive.

"See?" I turned to Stewart, who advanced on me like a purple-faced avalanche. I forced my face into a hopeful grin.

The rattling slither of chains sounded from inside the cannery, and I turned as a nauseous rush assaulted my senses.

I cried out in horror along with the bound men in the stockyard as oily, black chains burst through the windows in the central building. Like living things with hooked hands they plunged toward the men, snaring bonds, clothes, or flesh. It happened so quickly I hadn't even taken a breath before they were dragged, screaming, into the building.

"Bashir!?" Stewart asked, his ire gone, the colour draining from his face. "What the devil are you doing?"

"It wasn't me," I gasped. "I wouldn't..."

The screams inside the cannery stopped with sickening abruptness, and something else pressed on my awareness.

We stood beside the rusted framework of a truck bay. My gaze snapped upward to the exposed girders jutting from the blasted end of the cannery. My knees and stomach quailed as a red glimmer winked at me in time with another rush of putrid force. I felt the metal's despairing cry as the insidious corruption destabilised it, molecule by molecule.

"Run!" I screamed at the team as the girders reached critical mass.

The solid branches of steel had become bombs, shaped by the mad will of an ancient evil who would love nothing more than to see the whole world fester and die.

Hard-won instinct saved my life, as well as Stewart's.

I snatched up the last of the metal sheeting with my power and lifted it to block the sergeant and I from the blast. The sheet of tin slapped against us as thunder blasted, the force driving us to the ground hard, but sparing us from the worst of the explosion.

Our cheeks smashed into the dirt; the sergeant and I shared terrified looks under the shadow of our makeshift shield. As the ringing in my ears subsided, sporadic gunfire and screams filled them instead.

"G-et the team ou-t," I wheezed, fighting for each syllable as I struggled to catch my breath. Blood pounded through my head, making even my ears throb.

Stewart's face was pale, and every hard line in his craggy face seemed curled in fear. The shooting and the screams stopped abruptly. Something harder than any metal known to man flashed in Stewart's eyes.

"Bloody well dinna think so," he snarled. With a bellowing heave he threw the battered tin off.

We rose to our knees in an opaque curtain of dust and smoke. Stewart's eyes and rifle barrel swept around in frustrated defiance.

"Squad leaders, report," he growled. Static answered.

Somewhere in the fog, chains rattled.

I struggled to my feet, working on getting oxygen into my lungs. My metallic awareness was nearly as useless as the radio, overwhelmed by the feeling of wrongness in the fragments of metal swirling around us.

The chains clinked and rustled again, taunting.

"What are our options, Bashir?" Stewart continued his slow scan.

The dust cleared with unnatural slowness, cocooning us in a murky twilight.

"Let me clear the air." I reached my hands out to either side, laying a mental hold on the fluttering metallic dust. I winced at the contact of the befouled bits with my mind. The chains jangled irritably, and my skin prickled as the noxious aura bubbled up in my senses.

I swept my hands down, and the clouds sank to the ground.

In the devastated stockyard a monster clutched its prey with many hooked coils. The entire security team was bound. Vast lengths of greasy chains entangled them, hooks and many-toothed gears pressing just hard enough against throats, eyes, and groins, that not one moved.

"Let's not make a bad situation worse," drawled a familiar voice.

The head of the monster, leaning forward from the mass of metal like the figurehead of some infernal ship, was Dillon Sark, or something that had once been him. His frame was nearly skeletal now. His chest was a molten mass, seething and throbbing as metals wound over and through holes seared in flesh and bone. At a tone so low, I felt it as much as heard it, the demonic engine that was Kezsarak ground and thrummed.

*KILL HER*

I raised the battered tin, but Sark's strained laughter brought me up short.

"Mad ol' boy doesn't come with a mute button, I'm afraid," he said with a broad smile. His handsome features were ragged and painfully sharp, lips cracked raw, eyes fever bright. Life on the run had been hard on him, but life as a demon's vessel was eating him alive.

"Let them go 'fore I put a hole through your skull, lad." Stewart raised the rifle to his shoulder.

Sark's smile widened beyond human proportions, bones twisting like rubber.

With viperish speed, a length of chain whipped out and twisted around the sergeant, who roared in pain as it squeezed his arms to his sides. His rifle kicked off a single useless shot as it was slammed back against his chest.

Howling my defiance, I launched the sheet forward, sharpening the leading edge as it flew.

Sark sank deeper into the mass of chains and trapped soldiers. I couldn't hit him without slicing one of the security team open. I halted the tin and drew it back, letting it hover, ready to defend or attack.

"That's better," Sark cooed, sliding to the fore once more, though he kept his human shields close. "Now we can talk like civilised people."

In answer, I sheared my section of siding in half with a thought. One leaf moved in front of me, a rough shield, while the other hovered menacingly at my shoulder, a sharp projectile ready to fly.

"If you want to talk," I growled, setting my feet into a fighting stance, "then let them go."

Kezsarak's mechanical pulse quickened at the demand, sending a tremble through the chains. I prepared to defend and attack simultaneously, but his assault didn't come.

Sark eyed me. I'd spent enough time with him to be able read his face: he was afraid. He wasn't sure, even sharing a body and abilities with Kezsarak, that he could take me. Good. Let him doubt. I wasn't sure I could take him either, but I'd be damned before I'd let any uncertainty show.

"I will let them go." Sark's gaze swept over his captives with open contempt. "But first you need to listen."

I shuffled left and then right, looking for a way to get to Sark that didn't go through my team. "I'll listen if you let them go."

"Afraid not, lovely." He shook his head. "They're my insurance. Wouldn't want things to get ugly."

"Judging from what that demon's done to you, that's impossible." I gave him a pointed up and down.

"Not when she's still useful," Sark hissed, but not to me. He focused and smiled again. "Sorry about that. He's ... well, if anyone knows what he's like, it's you."

I kept my eyes fixed on his face, but a corner of my mind swept the area.

"For a bloke saying he wants to talk, you aren't saying much." I needed to keep his attention on me. "You went to all this trouble just to be cheeky? Is this your idea of flirting?"

"You're saying it isn't working?" Sark threw me a leering wink.

"We are far past that stage. You've gone insane, Sark, simple as that. You need to be stopped."

Sark's eyes widened with a burning light that would have made even an edimmu like Daria wince.

"Insane!" he snarled, spittle flecking his ravaged lips. "I'm following the plan! The plan that you could have helped me with!"

"You mean the plan to kill your way to Winterthür?" I retorted. "Yeah, wonder why I didn't sign up for that."

I felt a pair of metallic flickers in the wreckage behind him. I shifted, hoping to steal a peripheral glance. If he sensed me manipulating metal, my plan would be doomed.

"He's awake now." The pronouncement was flat and heavy.

"I know."

"If we had worked together, we could have stopped him," Sark said, his voice thick with sincere emotion. "Now that he is awake, the only way we can possibly survive is by working together."

"Not like this," I rasped. "Not your way."

Sark's eyes flashed, and the muscles in his jaw clenched. "It is necessary. What are a few lives to saving the planet?"

I met his grimace with a calm, steady voice. "That's not good enough," I said, appealing to whatever was left of this tortured creature's humanity. "A guardian doesn't sacrifice what they are meant to protect. I'm a guardian."

Sark's laugh was a jagged file across my nerves.

"You're a fool," he sneered. "Your high minded ideals will see the world burn!"

"Then I'll spend my last breath putting out fires."

The demoniac engine sounds grew more urgent and shrill. Sark shook his head viciously as the chains tightened fractionally. Every man in their grip held his breath, eyes wide.

I waited, inching over a little more.

"Let me handle this," he muttered out the corner of his mouth.

*KILL HER*

"Oh, shut-up!" Sark snapped. "A little patience wouldn't hurt you, you animal."

"Might hurt you, though," I deadpanned.

Launching my leaves of sheet metal, they flew through the air half a metre over Sark. As I expected, he shielded himself with my team – the poor wretches colliding with a clamour of metal links and wounded grunts. For a terrible instant, I feared I misjudged, but the metal cleared the men's heads by scant centimetres and sailed over Sark.

Sark didn't have time to consider his good fortune before the twin spines of rebar I'd spied behind him lanced into his back and dragged him into the air. His shock and Kezsarak's outrage kept him from mounting an effective defence, and with a heave of raw will I pulled him free of the chains.

The lengths of stained metal collapsed, limply hanging about their would-be victims.

I focused on pushing Sark up and away as quickly as I could. I felt the combined wills of Sark and Kezsarak pressing on the intersecting rebar, one trying to expel while the other began to violently dissolve them.

I drove my ringed fist up in a pantomime of an uppercut and sent them hurtling onto the roof of the cannery, landing with a crunch.

Summoning the twin leaves of sheeting back to me, I held them at my shoulders, ready to sweep down and block or lash out at a thought. I reached out to the lengths of chain not wholly compromised by Kezsarak's viral will, reinforcing the leaves with hardened folds and ridges. The extra links I spun out to encase my arms and shoulders in a metallic skin.

It wasn't perfect, but it would have to do. I didn't think for a second the fight was over.

Some of the team pointed at me, someone muttered the word "angel". I spared a look at the reshaped metal sprouting from my armoured shoulders. I hadn't intended it, but they did look like wings.

"What do we do, Bashir?" Stewart eyed the roof of the cannery as he moved to stand beside me.

"You need to run." Something shifted in the auras of metal within the cannery. I squared my shoulders.

"We've been over this," Stewart snorted. "Like bloody hell I'm leaving you."

I couldn't help but smile. The one time the crusty grunt treated me like one of his own and not baggage was the one time I needed him to drop me.

"There's nothing you have that can hurt him," I explained. "It's not Sark that will be coming now, but Kezsarak. Your weapons will only give him something else to hurt us with, and a stray shot could put me down. Simple as that, Sarge."

The chains in the stockyard shuddered and retracted into the cannery like a tide of clamouring, black snakes.

"Please." I took a step toward the looming industrial building, pulse picking up speed. "Help me by getting to safety."

Stewart ground his teeth loud enough to make my jaw ache, and then cursed as only a Scotsman could.

"Alright, lads," he bellowed, his face twisted like he'd swallowed a lemon. "You heard her. Hoof it!"

The security team had just cleared the yard when the roof of the cannery erupted. Stabbing up through the gaping wound was a nightmare of live metal and twisted hate. A serpentine trunk of jagged metal plates swivelled, a blunt head crowned in fused barbs revolved to face me. The head bloomed and out of its gaping throat came Sark's head and shoulders, but not his voice.

*NOW YOU DIE TRAITOR*

I didn't wait for the nightmare to come for me.

The wings clamped to my armoured shoulders, and with a surprisingly natural impulse I drove power into them. My feet came off the ground, and after a second of faltering, I let out a cry of terrified excitement.

I was flying! Flying to my death perhaps, but flying.

A wordless battle cry, something melodious and primal rose up in me as I surged forward to meet the demon's fury. The industrial worm lurched to meet my charge, bladed tines gnashing together in eagerness.

It was a game of chicken. With everything I had I thrust the jagged edges of my new wings forward and poured on more speed.

In the back of my mind, something bemoaned a foolish blaze of glory, but a burning elation drowned it out. Something like joy but brighter, harder, and more terrifying took the place of my heartbeat, and I was a speeding spear, an arrow loosed.

To my eternal surprise, the demon blinked. With a shriek of metal twisting against metal, the monster tried to turn away.

It was too late.

My lyric-less battle hymn crested as I plunged between the grasping barbs, my wings driving into Sark's shoulders. My momentum blasted out the back of the hellish construct's fused skull, and the whole thing began to crumble. Together we soared higher and pirouetted in the air.

Kezsarak's hateful spirit struck at me like poisoned claws, and I felt my wings succumbing to his rot.

*DIE*

"You first." I drove my ringed fist deep into his molten chest.

Pain--like fanged lightning--chewed its way up my arm, lunging toward my heart. Sark's head snapped back with an inhuman shriek, Kezsarak's bellow joining in.

I wrenched back, away from the excruciating pain, but my fist was lodged inside his chest. My screams joined the cacophony of sound as tongues of metal dragged my hand deeper. The metal encasing my limb began to glow. Heat built around my arm, soon to be scorching and unbearable.

Unable to free myself, and nearly blind with pain, I did the only thing I could: drove my fist deeper.

Things shifted and darted beneath the grinding pressure of my driving gauntlet. Pain and pressure increased. I ground my teeth and pushed deeper yet.

My knuckles pressed against his pulsing, metallic heart. Sensing the molecules of Kezsarak's rotting core coming apart, I opened my fingers to clasp his beating heart.

Then everything came apart in a flash of scouring light.

# TEN

I was falling.

A sulphurous sky hung above me as I plummeted. Something struck, causing me to roll and tumble; the world became a nauseous blur of sky and dark city below. My arms pinwheeled, I kicked at empty air, to no avail. My wings were gone, and my metallic sense felt nothing.

I was going to die. There was nothing I could do while falling from this kind of height; terminal velocity meant certain death.

I had long enough to wonder how I could be falling like this: Sark and I had only been thirty or so feet up. The surreal calm I felt at acknowledging my inevitable death combined with the absurdity of what would cause it stole over me. Laughing as you died didn't seem so bad.

There was a jolting shock as I struck the ground and rolled: shoulder-back-shoulder-stomach-shoulder three times over. I stopped, lying on one side on blurred grey stones. My stunned gaze followed the contours of distorted paving stones as they stretched into a narrow street that ran between insubstantial structures toward something huge and looming on the horizon. A lance of white light spiked into the dirty sky.

I am not sure how long I lay there, not daring to move, scared to even think for fear that the impact would catch up with me. Eventually, I raised my head in curiosity to watch the light's path into the heavens.

I sat up: not dead, and nothing wrong with my body. I clasped my hands to my knees, which seemed as solid as ever, and felt the hard surface beneath my body. I wondered how something which seemed so translucently out of focus could support me.

The light throbbed and I lost all interest in the composition of the street.

Still hardly believing that my legs worked, I stood and took a step. One foot followed another across the half-there stones, moving steadily toward the light. Partially formed thoughts surfaced – *where am I? where am I going?* – but they fell by the wayside as I trudged on.

A low-level anxiousness nagged at me, a fear that I was going to miss something. Every step I took was a short-lived salve against that nibbling awareness. I had to keep moving, getting closer to the light.

I could not miss it.

My peripheral vision registered the inane constructs of woven darkness on either side of the lane. Every so often something more tangible but just as dark would slither between the spun out blackness, but it did not keep me from walking.

I was closer, but the anxiety nagged that I could still miss it.

The street rolled on, perhaps rising in pitch by a degree or two, until I was close enough to see the source of the light.

A cyclopean presence, a mountain or pyramid of massive proportions squatted over the horizon. From its blunt crown, the light, so bright and beckoning, drove upward without a single flicker, a solid beam of raw energy.

I couldn't stop walking, didn't want to.

Closer, always closer.

I kept moving until the monolith, a mass of dark, glimmering gold, was all I could see. I had to strain my neck to see the light. A panicked thought: I would no longer be able to see the light once I reached the base. But a few steps later, I knew it'd be okay because I would be closer to the light, especially as I began to climb.

Closer.

Something intruded on my mind, a flicker of presence nudged against my awareness. A dissonant outburst of sound. I felt relief when it stopped, but it came again and again, battering its way into my consciousness.

"Ibby."

The auditory invasion made me cringe. I fought to ignore it; to keep moving closer, always closer, to the light… as a moth…

"Ibukun Bashir."

This longer assault was multipronged, gouging through layers of resistance into something that painfully resembled memory and thought. The rhythmic cycle of anxiety and soothing progression was crippled, the comfort stripped away.

"Ibukun Bashir, please!"

I needed it to stop, needed it to leave me alone. I whirled my arms, lashing out, turning away from the precious light for the first time in what felt like eternity. My fists beat against a body. A solid, familiar essence.

"Professor?"

The trance broke as I put my palms out on a set of narrow shoulders. Between my hands stood Professor James Lowe: friend, mentor, and incredibly distant relation.

"My dear Ibby." He almost sobbed as he drew me into a tight embrace. "Thank heavens. I thought you'd never respond."

I returned the hug, my mind still sluggish from the trance; but not too numb to notice that he felt as warm and pliant as any other person of flesh and blood. The implications of his sudden change from icy ectoplasm, or rather what I feared of my own change, filled my stomach with a cold soup of dread.

Lowe drew me back to arm's length, smiling until he saw my stricken expression.

"Ibby, what's wrong?"

"Am I ..." I found my mouth and jaw locked and my tongue reluctant to operate. I forced myself to swallow and began again.

"Am I dead?"

Lowe's eyebrows gathered in confusion over his sparkling grey eyes. The strange city around us, and the immense structure, seemed incredibly sinister now. How could I have been so attracted to such a malevolent construct? I moved my gaze back to Lowe and hoped something he said would keep me from collapsing.

He shook his head. "No. I don't believe you are."

I let out the breath I'd been unconsciously holding as a tremor of weary relief passed through me. My knees felt watery and my ankles wanted to roll. I picked up one foot and flexed it, then the other, finding strength again.

"Then where are we?" I stole a glance around and instantly regretted it. Between the glistening folds of midnight that made the buildings, things moved, twisted, and stirred.

"I am not sure." Lowe frowned as he looked around. "If I had to venture a theory, perhaps a dreamscape."

Two burning eyes glared at me from the darkness. I recoiled at the sudden expression of livid hate, and the motion drew Lowe's attention. He followed my gaze to the assemblage of midnight, eyes narrowing.

"Begone!" Lowe commanded in a voice more powerful than would have seemed possible for his lanky frame. "You have no business with us!"

The thing's liquid body squirmed in apparent displeasure, the eyes tightening into poisoned slashes of light. A sound like a cat issued from the shadows, then it was gone, lost in the frozen tides of black.

"What was that?" I shuddered.

Lowe shrugged after glaring into the darkness for good measure. "An evil shade or possibly a lesser demon."

"So... you just shooed away a demon?" I balked.

"Such beings are drawn to fear and weakness. In a dreamscape where the soul and mind form a fabricated reality, such beings hover like scavengers. If I showed it no fear, it should go off in search of easier prey."

I stared up at him, open-mouthed.

Lowe's pale features blushed, and he suddenly looked decades younger. He must have been striking, if not a classically handsome young man, once upon a time.

"Years of professional pedagogy has taught me that saying something with confidence, even if that something is utter idiocy, can accomplish a good deal. Self-possession is formidable, even if what hides behind it is bluster."

I surrendered a snort of laughter as I shook my head.

"Well done then, Professor." I smiled. "But if this is a dreamscape, it's not mine, and it doesn't seem to be yours."

Lowe's expression grew grave.

Another look up the face of the vast monolith I'd almost begun to climb filled my stomach with ice water. I didn't want to be in the dreams of anyone who populated it with such a strange and sinister landscape.

"So whose dream is it, and how did we get here?" I forced myself to lock onto Lowe's face before I saw more twisting shapes and burning eyes.

Lowe's lips tightened into a grim line. "Regardless of the identity of the dreamer, they are a being of singular power. The size of the dreamscape is one thing, but it pulled you, me, and Sark into it while vigorously conscious."

My body went rigid. "Sark's here?"

Tightening my hands into fists reminded me that I didn't have the Rings. They hadn't followed me into the realm of dreams, and now I felt exposed, vulnerable.

Lowe remained irritably calm in spite of our circumstances. "We were brought here together. If that other poor soul hadn't collided with you and sent you off course, you might have landed in the same place as Sark. I wouldn't worry about him, though. He seemed fixated on climbing that immense ziggurat, just like you were. I'm unaffected because I am a ghost."

"What other poor soul?"

"One of them." He pointed at the face of the brooding golden pyramid – ziggurat. I squinted up: dozens of people moved up glimmering steps carved into its face with a steady yet unrelenting pace that was hauntingly familiar.

"Who are they?" As I followed their progress I realised there were thousands of them. Various sizes, colours, and genders, but all moving upward, all moving closer to the beam of light at the top. An undercurrent of power tugged at my mind again, its steady pull a siren's song. Resisting it, I moved my gaze away from the light.

"They are Inconquo," Lowe said.

The proclamation was shock enough to draw my attention from the dreamscape's seductive gravity. I pivoted my gaze between Lowe and those climbing.

"So many," I breathed, the hair on the back of my neck spindling to standing. With a jolt like lightning through my gut, my eyes widened and I swept the assorted figures, looking for the form of a loved one.

"Is my uncle up there?"

Lowe's lip slid forward in a pensive pout. "I expect so."

Taking on what I thought of as his professorial stance, arms crossed, he continued. "Remember that the bloodline was founded thousands of years ago, it has had a long time to dilute. I doubt a tenth of them have the slightest idea that they are anything special. Of that tenth, excluding you and Sark, I would be surprised if more than half a dozen know they are Inconquo. Most experts in Near Eastern history consider the Inconquo a minor faction."

Watching the thousands of figures crawling up the side of the structure, a combination of awe and terror swept through me. Being an Inconquo had been a lonely business, even with Lowe as my mentor. Seeing that I was part of a family of thousands was both incredible and humbling, until I reached the terminus of the logic of why we were all here.

"Ninurta is the dreamer." It couldn't be anyone else. "Why has he brought us here?"

"I don't know," Lowe said. "But like Kezsarak's nocturnal attacks on you a year ago, I don't think Ninurta can do you any lasting harm in a dream. Even if it is his."

I shuddered as I remembered those terrible nightmares, veritable psychic assaults from the hateful demon. "Sorry, but that's not encouraging."

"It gets worse," Lowe continued. "Ninurta is much more powerful than Kezsarak. If he senses you resisting his call, he could turn his attention to you and hold your mind here for a very long time. I think it would be very bad if Sark was released before you."

My shoulders sagged. "You are saying I need to climb up there, aren't you?"

Lowe's face was grave, his eyes glistened with emotion.

"I'm afraid so, my dear."

My gaze swept the desolate, spectral city, and gave an angry laugh. "Then why go to the trouble of waking me out of that trance?"

Lowe placed a hand on my shoulder, his face heavy with sorrow. "I wanted you to know that you aren't alone."

---

THE TOP of the ziggurat was immense, a vast plateau that was both solid underfoot but also churned and seeped like molten gold. The expanse was filled with people who seemed somehow aware of my presence yet completely unconcerned with it. Their features remained indistinct with perpetually changing dream-like distortions, refusing to come into focus no matter how I strained my eyes. If they saw me as we saw them, Lowe and I were little more than mobile scenery. They were all gripped in Ninurta's trance anyway.

Vast concentric rings of people radiated outwards from a central pillar of light. It rose to impale the low, heavy belly of a sky the color of gunmetal. I stood at the edge of the plateau, one of the last to complete the climb, expecting to witness events from the periphery. Quietly, without a word, the crowd parted in a wave as those in the outermost ring shuffled a little to allow me to pass, as did those in the next and the next.

I felt the call to move inward; at first, I resisted, fearing that it would steal away my consciousness again. I wanted a better view of the proceedings, but not at the cost of my mind.

"I think we need to get closer," Lowe whispered in my ear. "I believe he is waiting for you."

"Why me?"

"You are the most powerful Inconquo to emerge in generations. I imagine that comes with a stronger connection to our progenitor."

I didn't like the sound of that, nor how Lowe referred to this psychotic maniac as our progenitor.

"Stay close," I muttered as I began to move through the rings of people.

As Lowe and I moved, a low, atonal buzz filled the air. At first, I took it to be a crackling discharge from the light, but it was coming from around us: words muttered under the breath of the multitude. Seriously creepy.

Halfway to the centre, and unexpectedly, the crowd scuttled together, separating Lowe and me. I tried to shove my way past the trance-locked people to get back to him, but my efforts were futile. It was not my will reigning here, that was clear.

"Go on," Lowe urged, hemmed in on all sides. "Remember, he can't hurt you. Not really."

I threw him my best jaunty salute, squared my shoulders and pressed forward. Lowe gave me an encouraging smile, nodding me forward.

As I trudged on, the whispers grew louder, words becoming recognisable as it rose into a droning chant.

"... to...founder...before... men... kings..."

Some spoke in languages I didn't recognize, yet with the prescient certainty of dreams, I knew what they meant anyway. The words were repeated, a litany looping over and over in a fraying, mind-numbing chant.

Reaching the central rings which basked in the glow of the pillar of light, I slipped between light lined silhouettes, catching glimpses of the heart, the something from which the light rose.

"...hail to him... first founder of... before him all despair... slayer of men... of kings..."

My mouth began to form the words of the chant. I clamped my jaw shut so hard that my molars clicked together. I'd be having none of that. I shook my head to clear the fog creeping at the edges of my consciousness.

Another break in the ring ahead of me, too far to the left to reach, caught my attention. It was hard to get a better look, the entranced people always shuttling me inward, but I managed to twist around one of them to see the reason for the break.

Dillon Sark—in his human form--crouched on the ground, one hand bracing his weight while the other clawed feebly at a dark spidery fist wrapped around his throat. The hand belonged to a body of living shadow, not much bigger than a toddler but with long arms and legs out of proportion to its small body. With one hand, it throttled Sark until his face turned purple, while with the other hand it stroked his cheek in a perversely intimate gesture.

The chanting had grown loud enough that I had to shout, but I tried to draw the wicked-looking apparition's attention.

"Leave him alone!"

Sark probably deserved to die, but not like this.

"Get off him!"

The wicked thing's oddly angular head perked up and with a boneless twist turned to regard me. Eyes like ingots pulled from a blast furnace burned in my direction, and I heard the familiar sound of Kezsarack's roaring, mechanoid voice.

*END THIS*

"What are you doing to him?" I yelled back. "You're killing him."

*GO*

With that, Kezsarak returned his attention to Sark, who trembled and gasped on his knees. I couldn't help him. Feeling sick to my stomach, I turned back to the next open passage leading through to the rings.

Taking a steadying breath, I stepped forward through the final two layers of Inconquo, determined to walk unflinching toward whatever Ninurta had in store for me. A wind whipped up, pulling at my clothes, as thunder rumbled in the churning, brimstone clouds overhead.

Planting one foot in front of the other, but making certain that I did of my own free will, I reached the darkened throne of Ninurta, the First Inconquo. To my horror, I raised my head and proclaimed, louder than any of those I'd passed, the chant that had been worming its way into my mind.

"Ninurta, king of kings, all hail him the first founder of cities, before him all despair of their mighty works, for he is builder and slayer of men, gardener and hunter before the face of god is he, Ninurta, king of kings."

# ELEVEN

With my unwilling proclamation the brilliant beacon that had drawn all the Inconquo to this place retreated. Like a waterfall of starlight, it flowed down into a throne, awakening a fire within. The jagged assortment of cold, black slag began to flow and roil, becoming a throne of liquid metal held together by the will of the one who sat upon it.

I averted my eyes from the glow of the throne, fearing what new spell I would be under if I looked at him.

"Come now, my child." The voice was rich and deep, and as terrible as time itself. "Look upon your father and be made new."

My eyes betrayed me.

Ninurta was both less and more than I imagined. Reclining upon his throne was a huge but emaciated figure of bygone majesty and power. The rich fabrics that flowed around him were threadbare, and the jewellery that seemed to drip from every part of him was dull and tarnished. Thick ropes of muscle still corded his frame, but they moved beneath weathered, wrinkled skin, and his broad back was bent. His hair and beard were white and in places worn so thin that liver-spotted skin could be seen beneath. His chestnut eyes were bright with watchful intelligence, but even they seemed to sag with the incredible weight of long, long years.

He was an old king, a man nearing the end of his reign.

Seeing him like that filled me with an odd combination of sorrow and joy. An old and mighty creature nearing its end was always sad, but his apparent infirmity led me to believe that perhaps there was yet hope he could be defeated. I had been raised to respect my elders, but in the case of my maniacal demigod progenitor, I would make an exception.

"You are smiling," he observed, his voice filled with interest. "What do you see?"

I hadn't realised I was smiling, but I wasn't about to back down. I was pretty sure that if I did, I would crumble. He might be an ageing king, but his presence and will were still incredibly potent.

"I see an old man." I forced my voice to be steady in a way that my knees were not. "Powerful and dangerous, but still old."

Ninurta nodded, the motion all the more sagacious for his swaying grey hair.

*Grey? Hadn't his hair been white? Why couldn't I see through to his spotted scalp anymore?*

A sick feeling crept into my stomach. Was he changing before my eyes?

"Oh, but I am old." His heavy brows slid low, turning his look crafty. "But it is one of the great follies of the young to think age makes one impotent."

I stared up into his face, refusing to be cowed. "And it is the folly of the old to think the young are incapable."

"Such would be true if you faced anyone else," he said tenderly. A patronising smile spread across the aged face, as though he was explaining something to a child. "Your spirit does you credit. In my new world, I wish to foster exactly that kind of daring."

His dark eyes glittered in wizened sockets, but the folds about them weren't as heavy now.

"You got that from me, you know." His hands hung from the armrests of his seething throne. Two fingers on his left hand were made of gold – digits of living metal.

"We may be separated by epochs but it is true," he continued. "More than anything, these long years have given me perspective, and with that perspective, I see *you*. Can you see *me*?"

The last word rippled through the air like the distortions rolling off a furnace; for an instant I felt his will and I couldn't suppress a shudder. Monstrous in size and scope, he was a psychic leviathan in whose wake I could barely keep from being dragged along. Lowe had promised he couldn't hurt me, but I wasn't so certain.

"You begin to understand." He grinned, shark-like, and his potent aura swept by me again. A small, weak sound escaped my lips as I fell to my knees, shaking.

Kezsarak's power, both bound within Sark and unfettered, had been ferocious and relentless. This was something else, something I couldn't have imagined until I'd experienced it. Now that I had, I felt diminished and cold.

"What are you?" I gasped, tears springing to my eyes.

In answer, Ninurta rose, his back straightening as the guise of infirmity sloughed off him. Muscles swelled to fill glistening skin, while his hair and beard shone jet black and lustrous. He stepped down from the throne with a dancer's lithe movements. He was a warrior king in his prime, a sorcerous monarch at the height of his power.

"I am the first, and I am the only," he intoned as he advanced. "I am the culmination of the grand design. I was a child among grunting brutes when I first understood that I was destined for more."

He stared out at the dream horizon as though he might see those bygone days there, playing out on the sky. I remained on my knees, watching him, gathering the courage I felt I might be losing at being so near him.

"By the will of nature or god, I rose from that savage beginning with not just dreams and ambitions, but the power to achieve them. Whatever I laid my hand to was mine, mastery was my birth right. While my tribe cowered in caves and scratched out their living amongst stones, I learned the mysteries which lay beneath the earth."

His gaze returned to me, and I marvelled to see tears glittering at the corners of his eyes.

"I returned to them," he said softly. "The simple creatures from which I emerged. I strove to teach them, but they were too simple, too crude. They turned on me, fearing what I'd become."

He closed his eyes, drawing in a heavy breath. When he continued, his voice was flat and cold.

"I killed them all. It broke my heart, but in my agony, as I throttled the last of the misbegotten children, I had a revelation: some are incapable of ascendancy, and their very existence holds back those who would climb up to pluck the stars."

He swept around in a slow circle viewing his children arrayed about him. The rings of dreaming Inconquo began their chant again, low and urgent.

My voice surged to join them, but I forced my jaws together until I thought they would break, refusing to submit. Disgust at the display of vacancy and submission rose like bile in my throat.

"I determined to build an empire, a dynasty where the exceptional might ascend. I founded Kalhu and set about uniting man under my name. But again they disappointed me. They sought to worship gods and such smallness disgusted me. Had I not slain enough of their demons for them to see what they could become if they only willed it? I watched factions spread through my house and came to hate my children; I grew weary of waiting for mankind to evolve enough to suit my purpose. So I decided to sleep, to dream away the ages. I just needed someone to ensure I was not disturbed until the time was right."

Thunder crashed and lightning crackled above us. The dream wind was rising as though to dramatize his story.

"I found a creature as eternal as I: the edimmu that Lamashtu sent to kill me. With her phylactery held in the balance, I enlisted her to seal my tomb and hold the key for a time. Until the world could be shaped to my will. She despised her corrupted condition, so I knew eventually she would awaken me hoping to end her own cursed existence. But lo, I am awakened, and the fallen priestess has done well. This world is ready at last."

The chant rose, beating against me like waves, making every thought a struggle, but I knew who he meant: Daria. Her part in this distressing story fit so many pieces together, but it was little comfort. It seemed like we were all doomed, Inconquo and edimmu alike.

"Ready for what?" I was not sure I wanted to hear the answer.

"Rebirth. To be broken open and reformed. I shall reach to the very heart of the world using the resonance of my descendants – now as many as the sands across the world. It will then be a simple matter to build a new world order."

With growing horror, I began to understand: the earth's heart, its core, is hypothesised to be metal. His plan seemed insane – changing the movements of the earth's core could bring about untold destruction – but the sanity of the plan didn't matter if he could actually accomplish it.

"That will kill millions of people," I cried.

Ninurta corrected me blithely. "I am told that the teeming masses count in the billions now, and by my calculations the initial casualties will be forty percent."

I stared at him, unsure how to even speak to someone who could say this with such calm.

"Come now, child, you've surely learned of the way of nature. It is only natural that unsuitable creatures perish and those worthy of life rise to prominence. I will merely accelerate the process. Evolution is imprecise, but the truth will out eventually; and when it does, I will be there to usher the worthy into a golden age that will never end."

The magnitude of his insanity was mind-numbing. I suddenly felt like I was drowning and needed to push away from the suffocating weight of his vision, to bring things back to a scale I could understand.

"So what do you want with me then?" I shouted to be heard over the rising chorus. "Why this whole production?"

Ninurta's brows rose, a shadow briefly passing over his face before he knelt in front of me, bringing me to my feet. His huge hands took mine in a firm but gentle grip. He on his knees, and I on my feet, we were eye-to-eye; and snared in those deep, dark pools, I couldn't move.

"I want you to join me, child." His voice was quiet but impossibly clear through the tumult. "You, whether through will or destiny have risen above any who came before you. I am determined to never need an heir, but it would please me to have you at my side, adding your strength to mine in this great work. Be my princess, be my consort, be my queen, be whatever you will, but be so with me. Let us remake the world together."

I stared at him, wind tugging at my hair as the sky threatened to tear itself apart.

The offer, as abhorrent as it was, still had temptation – not least because I knew Ninurta would not take rejection well. The idea of such power for a girl who'd spent her life scuttling along the bottom of the proverbial barrel was incredible. Looking at Ninurta's bright eyes and soulful expression, I could almost convince myself that with time and tact, I could influence him. Wasn't it better to guide such power?

One look around me answered that question. Thousands of his descendants enslaved in his dreamscape, chanting his praises. Ninurta was a force of nature, a malevolent tidal wave, either I rode with him into destruction pretending I was in control, or I stood in defiance.

*I am a guardian.*

"No," I met his gaze levelly. "I won't join you. Not now, not ever."

He was composed in the face of rejection. "Oh, my dear, you don't even know what I am going to do. It will be magnificent."

I shook my head, refusing to look away. "I've heard fanatics muttering doomsday prophecies: the world made new as the wicked are destroyed and the faithful rewarded. I will not be part of your apocalypse."

Ninurta frowned and stroked his beard thoughtfully.

"If apocalypse is what I bring, then you will be bound up in it, like it or not." A genial grin lit his face. "But you mustn't take those poor souls too seriously. They're pawns, not princes. It is their place to serve, and be sacrificed for the good of better men."

Now it was my time to smile, grim and hard to match my voice.

"And that right there, is why my answer is never. They aren't pawns to be cast aside, but people who need to be protected."

The skies shivered as rivers of lightning coursed searing tracks overhead. Something hard and ugly appeared in the king's gaze before it sank deep into eyes growing watery with sad resignation.

"I hoped this wouldn't happen." He got up and walked toward his throne, his movements weary, as though bearing a heavy burden. "I'd hoped that whatever had made me had resurfaced in you."

He settled into place with a ponderous elegance. Even knowing what he was, he looked noble, as though stoically shouldering the weight of ruling on his broad, sculpted shoulders.

"I had expectations, but I will wait a little longer for one who has awoken to the same truth I have."

The spell broke on the word 'truth'. He really saw himself as the tragic hero, and somehow knowing that fractured whatever glamour he'd woven over me. He was a self-pitying monster, no matter how he dressed it up.

My lip curled. "You're breaking my heart, but if it means you're going to crawl back into your metal box and sleep another few millennia, then I'm all for it."

Ninurta stared at me for a few heartbeats, and I looked right back, my chin thrust out. I'd chosen defiance and I would give it my all.

Something passed between us that told me he knew what I'd seen. His wickedness, his selfishness, his madness.

"There is no turning back after this," he said. "Once I end this dream, there will be no conversation, no parley, no second chances." His voice grew colder, sharper with every syllable.

"Promise?" I asked in an exaggeratedly hopeful voice. "Cross your heart and hope to die?"

"Very well." He looked down his nose, not amused. "Ibukun Bashir, once the bright hope of a degenerate generation, I declare you my enemy and unworthy of the blood you carry in your veins. I shall come for you. I will not suffer the insult of my children's defiance."

Ninurta gave a dismissive flick of his hand.

"Take her from my presence."

Hard hands grabbed my arms and hauled me backward. More gripped my throat, my legs, and my waist. My first instinct was to scream in outrage, but I reminded myself this was a dream. *You can't hurt me. This is a dream. Only a dream.* My mind whispered reminders to my heart to keep it from pounding itself into a panic. The murky-faced figures in the innermost ring carried me away from the throne, and I let them, focusing on keeping the fear they wanted to incite at bay.

They dragged me closer to the next circle where they squeezed and wrenched at my limbs and body, passing me to the hands of the next ring. My world became a suffocating tide of rough fingered and sharp nailed hands, dragging me away in the cruellest way possible, away from the throne and toward the ziggurat's edge.

With the surety of a dream I knew what they intended, and just as surely, I surrendered to the oppressive current.

*It is just a dream.*

That became my mantra...until I was plummeting, screaming, toward the shadow-swathed city below.

# TWELVE

A churning, humming sound grated on my frayed nerves but the hands were still there, though perhaps not as many. I loosed an enraged scream.

"Get off me!"

"For god's sake, hold 'er down!"

The grips tightened, but so did my resolve to escape.

The world was a blur of colours that didn't make sense, but I sensed open space to my right and hurled myself toward it.

Profanity-laden cries erupted. Hands lost their grip, and my feet hit solid ground. I shrieked a defiant victory, dragging those I couldn't twist away from as I tried to run.

"Ibby, please stop!"

I knew that voice, but when massive arms wrapped around my body, engulfing me until I was sure I would be crushed to death, the primal will to fight, to escape, to survive, overcame me. I heard grunts of pain as I fought, but the grip held.

Eventually I collapsed, exhausted, my rage expired. The forced embrace didn't withdraw, but as my legs gave way I was lowered into a sitting position. By degrees the arms loosened, slabs of muscle slowly relaxing. As the constricting force lessened, the fog of the nightmare and claustrophobia dissipated. The world began to make sense again.

I was high up, overlooking London. The sky was indigo with bands of violet and the city glittered with a million lights. A second longer and I recognised the whirring sound, now slowing and fading: as helicopter blades. Understanding crashed over me. The dream was over. I was still alive. I was seated on the rooftop helipad of The Nakesh Corporation building, less than a metre from the edge.

I shuddered at what had almost happened – my dream becoming reality – and unconsciously pressed myself against the broad chest that braced me.

"Can I let go now?" Marcus's voice was breathy from his exertions. "Or are you going to go mad again?"

"I think I'm good," I whispered, "but that doesn't mean you should let go."

The second he let go, everything would come crashing back in and a new kind of madness would take hold. What had I done, defying such a force as Ninurta? Even taunting him. Had I gone momentarily nuts inside that dream? It was like I'd had a death-wish. Strangely, I was more afraid now than when I had been inside that nightmarish dreamscape.

"Okay," he whispered back and pulled me in closer. "Have it your way."

The wind was cold, but Marcus was warm against me. He shifted his position and slid his thick legs alongside mine, a protective shield. I rested my head against his chest and savoured the steadying rhythm of his breathing.

"Can you tell me what happened?" he asked after a long while and our hearts returned to a normal rhythm.

"I met Ninurta," I croaked, licking at dry lips.

Marcus tensed, but to his credit he waited, letting me share in my own time.

"He pulled me into a dream. One he created with his mind, but it was so real, Marcus. Full of zombie Inconquo worshipping him." I shuddered with disgust.

"That sounds ... terrifying." Marcus slid his hand up and down my arm in soothing strokes. "Why did he bring you there?"

"To recruit me."

The city lights blurred into a kaleidoscope of dancing glows.

"He thought I'd be tempted to join his legion of doom as queen of his new world order." I could hardly say the words without nausea closing off the back of my throat.

Marcus took in a heavy breath and then let it out slowly.

"Then he really doesn't know you. Such goodness as you have is foreign to him." He kissed the side of my head.

Love surged through my heart for the man cradling me, his utter faith that I would do the right thing. Mingled with that affection was a touch of shame and I let out a long exhale, feeling my heart throb. Could I ever fully be who my sweetheart thought I was? I hadn't the heart to tell him that I had in fact been momentarily tempted, even if I had been in a trance.

"I hope you told him where he could stick his offer." Marcus chuckled: a warm, buttery sound that made me want to melt in his arms and be cradled there forever.

I nodded against him and he kissed my cheekbone.

"He didn't take it well." I said, feeling a little bit of the cold creeping in. The wind was picking up. "Said he was coming for me."

The muscles enfolding me quickened, ridges of indignation flexing. Muscular strength would be useless against Ninurta, but right now, holding me like he was, it was a kind of magic to soothe my soul.

"Things are about to get worse, aren't they?" Concern thickened his voice.

"Much worse, at least for me." Ninurta had promised to come for me.

There was a long pause, only his steady breathing and the wind broke the silence.

"You aren't alone," Marcus whispered in to the nape of my neck. "Please, remember that."

I looked out over my beautiful city and envisioned the kind of ruin Ninurta could bring to the glittering, metal-boned landscape. I saw the Gherkin folding in on itself as people screamed and fled, the Shard bifurcating to plunge like two titanic blades on the wailing masses. Death, chaos and ruin to appease the mad narcissist.

I could see the truth of what needed to happen. For a guardian there was no other choice.

"I'm not alone right now. And that's enough."

---

"I NEED to face Ninurta on my own."

I sat in Marks' office with Stewart, both of us cleaned up but looking the worse for wear. Stewart's eyes were haunted, and his craggy face seemed gaunt. I looked even worse. We'd concluded the debrief; Stewart had filled in the missing pieces about separating me from Sark after we plummeted to earth, while I explained about the dreamscape. Now we were discussing the next step.

"Is this some sort of warrior code, soldier's honour, nonsense?" Marks turned a withering look on Stewart.

The sergeant gave me a side-long glance as he squirmed uncomfortably in his chair.

"I dinna think that's the case, mum. I ken Ms Bashir's reason, though god knows it hurts me. She wants to do this on her own because ... well, because we're no use to her in this fight."

It felt wrong to nod my head at an admission that probably cost Stewart more than I could appreciate, but it was true. I mouthed thank you as Marks spun away to prowl around her desk.

Stewart gave me a short nod, his eyes soft. The soldier finally understood our respective places in this fight.

"I don't invest so much in an asset just to let that asset engage in a suicide mission," Marks remarked coolly, turning her gaze to me. "I didn't get this far wasting resources."

It was chilling to realise that was how Marks saw me: an asset, a resource. I supposed she had to view people like that to keep from being crippled by the emotional turmoil of making tough decisions, but still ... damn.

"We need to limit the damage," I explained. "If Ninurta comes for me while I'm in London, he'll bring carnage on an incredible scale and there will be nothing any weapons can do. In fact our weapons would only become fodder for his assault. I need to be somewhere he won't be able to hurt anyone but me."

Marks frowned, arms crossed, tapping manicured nails on her silver-grey jacket.

"Do you really believe he'd be that reckless?" she asked. "Would he disregard the secrecy so valuable in this business?"

"This isn't business to Ninurta." I leaned forward to emphasise my point. "This is destiny. He's not going to be subtle. He once ruled the world, or close to it, and he plans to do so again. He doesn't care about secrecy because he plans for the majority of the population not to be here anymore."

Marks blinked, paling. "And how exactly is he going to do that?"

I took a deep breath, knowing that this part wasn't going to be easy to swallow.

"Ninurta plans to somehow harness the power of his many descendants to affect the earth's metal core. The incredible destruction will jump-start a contest for survival. The winners of that contest, superior humans, in his eyes, will be the foundation of his new empire."

"These are the ravings of a madman," Marks said with a shake of her head. "I need actual intelligence."

"Insane or not, it would be stupid to underestimate both his conviction and his power."

"And facing him alone doesn't strike you as underestimating your opponent?" Marks asked, cocking one eyebrow. "This isn't some spaghetti western where good and evil square off to decide the fate of the common folk."

"I'm not doing this because I think I can beat him," I answered, folding my hands in my lap so she couldn't see my fingers tremble. "This is about damage control, pure and simple. Every minute he spends focused on me is time you can use to secure as many Inconquo as you can. If we can keep them out of his grip, maybe we can stop him."

"*You* were the way to stop him!" Marks's face scrunched into a snarl. "*You* are the weapon we were supposed to wield against him!"

Marks' words cut, but I wouldn't let her see that. She hadn't met Ninurta, she had no idea what we were facing.

"I am not enough." I replied, my voice quiet. "For better or apocalyptic worse, I'm a shield, a guardian, not a weapon. That may not be enough to stop Ninurta, but I can slow him down, so that is what I intend to do."

Her eyes narrowed, and her lips pressed together into a tight line.

"I could stop you." She spoke so softly that I struggled to hear her. "Detain you until I found some way to *encourage* your compliance."

My hackles rose; a rush of anxious, violent energy drove me out of my seat, to stand eye-to-eye, matching the older woman's glare.

"Steady now, Bashir," Stewart warned.

The Rings quickened in my hand, responding to my heightened emotions. I ground my teeth and set my jaw against a hundred angry words that ran circuits in my mind.

"You could," I said, carefully forming each word. "But that would be a waste of the limited time and resources you have. If you try to keep me here you are calling destruction down upon London. Let me go and I can give you time. You have several brilliant strategic minds here at TNC, employ *them* in the time that I'll make for you."

Marks stared at me for several agonising seconds. I waited, somehow feeling that was improper to look to Stewart for a sign.

"We have access to Otterburn in Northumberland." Marks' shoulders sagged a little, her voice worn and brittle. "We'll arrange transport and put the word out that you are training there. It is secluded. I don't imagine you'll have to be up there for long if Ninurta is as hot on your heels as you say he is."

"Thank you." It seemed an odd thing to say to someone letting you go on a suicide mission, but I was thankful for her acceptance.

"Don't thank me." She waved a hand. "I'm just being pragmatic."

I nodded, feeling a pang of pity for the defeated tone in her voice.

"What is Otterburn?" I asked. "A game reserve or national park?"

"It's an ATE, Army Training Estate," Stewart said as he heaved himself out of his chair. "Sees regular use by the military, but I'm sure Marks can pull the strings necessary to see you're not disturbed."

Marks didn't bother to comment. She'd swung her chair to look out the window, putting her back to us.

"Could you give me a map and details of the layout?" I asked.

Stewart nodded and motioned toward the door.

"I'll make sure you're as briefed as you can be, dinna worry aboot that."

Stewart and I moved toward the office door.

"Ibby." Marks called while still facing her window.

I paused, one hand on the doorknob. "Yes, ma'am?"

Marks drew in a breath, squaring and straightening her shoulders. She turned to face me and her voice was as clear as the first day I'd met her.

"Make the bastard work for it."

---

MARCUS THUMPED his bag down next to mine. "I'm coming."

Gritting my teeth as I rammed the last of my clothes into a rucksack TNC had issued me, I sent a glare his way. I had known this was coming. I wanted to both hug and throttle him for it.

"What's next, you going to offer my uncle ten goatskins for me to have your babies?"

Marcus leaned against the wall and smirked.

"We won't live long enough for that," he remarked dryly. "But if we somehow make it that far, I'll start the negotiations at twelve goatskins. Exorbitant I know, but you're worth it."

I growled when the pack refused to close.

"So I suppose you think it's chivalrous to go behind my back, to get your way?"

"Hardly." He shrugged. "You get to make plans without talking to anyone; I get to make plans without talking to anyone. It's called equality."

The pack finally closed, and I whirled on him. Fear for his life surged around in my stomach, sloshing like too much water. "Isn't this hard enough, already?"

Marcus's face softened as he pushed away from the wall.

"I'm not trying to make this harder. I can't do much to *help* you, but I can be *there* for you. So you don't face this alone."

Some of the frustration drained out of me, my heart softening. Marcus met me in a hug.

I closed my eyes and replayed my goodbyes to Jackie and Uncle Iry. I'd told them I was going to Otterburn to set a trap for the demigod, but I'd downplayed the danger and hadn't told them I'd be doing it alone. They thought I'd be going with the usual TNC legion. By the time I'd kissed them goodbye, they still hadn't known the possibility that we'd never see one another again. I couldn't have borne the anguish of a true goodbye, so I hadn't told them about the dreamscape, the true power of the enemy.

I held Marcus close to me. I would never get him to stay behind. He knew too much. He'd stick to me like a burr until I left the building. I'd just have to do my best to protect him. I released him and snatched up my bag. Too much time to think in circumstances like these wasn't a good thing.

"Let's go then."

# THIRTEEN

The first night at Otterburn ATE--a bleak and scruffy plain with the occasional copse of trees and knobby hill--was a sleepless one.

We'd settled in one of the small utility sheds and I tried to explain to Marcus why I wanted to draw Ninurta here.

"I want a level playing field. I'm pretty sure he could rip skyscrapers from the ground to throw at me, but out here he can only use metal on same the scale as myself."

Marcus looked around the shed, which housed a few dusty toolboxes and a couple of small tractors that looked like they had been old when Margaret Thatcher had been Prime Minister.

"Assuming that he doesn't bring his own skyscraper to throw at you."

We lapsed into brooding silence which eventually led to a fitful sleep.

When the sun rose we emerged from the shed, our eyes bloodshot and our shoulders drooping. Birds twittered morning songs, dew glittered on the grass. All was peaceful serenity.

We splashed water on our faces and brushed our teeth using a half cup of water from our supply. I stretched at the open door of the shed, working the kinks out of my back and shoulders from sleeping on a thin mat on the hardpacked dirt floor.

"All is quiet on the western front," I said, grabbing my foot and stretching out my quad. The rings hugged my fingers, warm and ready for when I'd need them... which appeared to be not as soon as I'd thought.

"I guess he's not in that big of a rush," Marcus murmured as he rummaged for a coffeemaker and the necessary sundry in the back of the shed on a makeshift desk. He made coffee using a propane hot-plate and an old-fashioned espresso maker while I wandered the grounds, making note of landscape features and watching for signs of the mad demigod. By the time I returned to the shed, Marcus was waiting with a steaming cup of very strong java. The warmth and the caffeine were both welcome.

"So, are we just going to sit around and wait for him to show up?" Marcus asked, taking a sip from his cracked mug.

I smiled and blew the steam off my own cup. "Not quite."

I told him what I had in mind.

• • •

NINURTA ARRIVED THE NEXT DAY, but I was certain of his arrival when I woke that morning.

Our insane scheme was ready, after much sweat and toil. He and I had spent the second night together on two thin camping rolls laid out side by side: his arms around me, my head on his powerful chest, I actually rested, feeling a peace I'd not known in months. When I woke to pale sunlight slanting in through the dusty windows, I spent a perfect moment looking at the man who loved me first and who had proved it over and over.

Until an unwelcome voice intruded on my loving thoughts.

*I come for you tonight, little one.*

I felt his malignant presence roll in like a black cloud over the face of the new-born sun. A chill ran through me and my shivering woke Marcus.

"What is it?" He came wide awake almost immediately. "What's wrong?"

"He's coming." I tucked my face against his throat.

Should I thank Ninurta for having the courtesy to warn me so clearly? Was it a rule of his sick game? The fact that I knew when he'd come only filled me with dread. He wanted me to be prepared, I'd put up a better fight that way. He didn't just want to destroy me and be done with it, he wanted a battle. Fury surged through me and I ground my teeth. I'd give him a battle alright.

Marcus's whole body tensed and he held me tighter. "When?"

"Tonight."

"You're ready." Marcus kissed my head and didn't question how I knew, just believed me. Oh how I loved him for that. "We're ready."

"I hope so."

"I know so."

---

Snow fell that afternoon and the night was bitterly cold, but the ground was bright with reflected moonlight.

Ninurta came out of the east like an ill wind of ancient texts, but instead of riding upon storm clouds, he came in a large black helicopter. I was a little disappointed given the build-up. At least he could have leaped out of the helicopter mid-air to land in some dramatic pose.

I gave my metallic wings a little flex. I'd expanded on the impromptu idea from Spain by adding a second set. All four were folded on my back, looking like an odd backpack.

The first passenger to emerge was not Ninurta, but a heavyset man wearing what looked like an electrician's utility coveralls. After him came a petite woman in fashionable but weather-inappropriate top and slacks. Half a dozen others emerged: men and women of varying sizes, shapes, and colours. All had the same expression of rapture on their faces, zealous and terrified.

They formed a rough column by the open door of the helicopter, each one turning to stare eagerly back the way they'd come. A large shape loomed in the opening, and a tremble raced up my legs; it took everything I had to force it down.

Ninurta was immense beyond what seemed humanly possible, towering over his entourage. Like in the dream, he moved with unnatural grace, stepping onto the ground so lightly I was surprised he left prints in the snow.

But not everything was the same as the dream.

The open chested robes and silken train had been replaced by a dark suit cut to accentuate every brutal and majestic angle of his frame. His hair and beard were much shorter, still glossy and luxuriant but without gold or silver adornments; however, his two fingers still glittered solid gold. He looked ready to run a board meeting. Treading through the snow, every movement was confidence and authority.

"Took you long enough," I shouted over the dying helicopter engines.

"You may be in a hurry to die," Ninurta said, his voice carrying perfectly without needing to be raised. "But I am in no great rush to end your life, my child. I do this because I must, not because it gives me pleasure."

I didn't believe that for a second.

He advanced past his line of ogling admirers, who fell in behind him. I forced my gaze to stay locked on his face. I needed to keep him talking, keep him walking toward me.

"Why bring an entourage?"

Ninurta raised his hand, and they stopped in their tracks. He took another step forward.

"They wanted to be here." He swept his arm back toward them. "These are a few of those who did not turn down my invitation. They wished to bear witness to my judgement, yes, but also to show you that they serve of their own free will."

I scoffed openly, shaking my head before turning my gaze to look at each moon-eyed face. Free will, my arse.

Beyond those I could see, more moved through the fringes unseen, I could sense the metal weapons they held. Those had not been delivered by a helicopter or I would have seen them. Perhaps delivered by a vehicle then, dropped off far enough away that we'd not heard the engines. My senses sharpened and my heart rate jumped but I kept an outward appearance of knowing calm.

"I don't know what you do to them," I crossed my arms, "but a bunch of pining groupies isn't going to convince me that you're anything but a dime-a-dozen cult leader. You look the part, but you're still nothing but a conman who's bought his own line."

The zealots responded with a chorus of angry, indignant sounds in several languages and began to shuffle forward.

"Peace," their idol called over his shoulder, and like he'd cast an enchantment, they went back to adoring him.

"You talk as one who is holding the moral high ground," he observed, taking yet another step, "but who goes to train under the watchful eye of four assassins? Did you really think to lure me here so I could fall to cowards shooting from behind bushes and rocks?"

I straightened with surprise, realization sliding through my mind like a razor's edge. Those moving through the fringes were not his, they were ours. Up until that moment I had believed that TNC had sent me and Marcus up here alone. Marks, in some desperate bid, had sent sharpshooters in hopes of ending this nightmare with a sniper's bullet. That was annoying and not at all what we'd agreed. She'd only put more people in danger.

"I didn't invite them," I said, trying to sound nonchalant.

Ninurta laughed, a rolling sound of liquid mirth. "No need to worry. As we flew in, I made certain they will not interfere."

He took another step and raised a hand to his ear dramatically.

"Listen." He turned left and right in mock anticipation.

A second later, there were three sharp cracks from among the hills followed by a crunching rumble like distant thunder. In the echoing stillness that followed, a single, pain-riddled shriek carried over the snow. Every hair stood on end at the sound.

"That was the sound of sniper's rifles suffering catastrophic failures," Ninurta declared, turning back to me with a sharkish grin. "Now, it's just you and me, my dear."

A hummock of earth just behind the demigod exploded with flying snow. Emerging from the eruption like a muscle-bound jack-in-the-box was Marcus, a loop of rope clutched in both hands. With a speed that belied his bulk, he threw himself on the giant, just managing to slip the noose around Ninurta's neck and cinch it tight before Ninurta spun with feline agility. One hand blurred out and Marcus was spun like a top before crashing to the ground poleaxed.

"Marcus!" I screamed even as I launched a dart of will to flatten the wedge restraining a trio of man-thick logs. There was a slow, creaking groan as potential energy became kinetic energy and they rolled down the steep slope.

Ninurta was hauled backward with bone-snapping force as the rope attached to his noose followed the logs. I'd dared to hope the force would snap his neck, but I saw his fingers rake deep grooves in the snow before he vanished over the cusp of the hill.

I rushed to Marcus.

He was on his hands and knees, blood flowing freely from his nose and mouth.

"Are you alright?" I asked, kneeling in the snow next to him.

I eyed Ninurta's followers warily: wide-eyed and motionless. Without orders, they were useless.

"I'm fine." Marcus spat, streaking the snow with blood as he fought to climb to his feet. With one hand he gripped my arm to steady himself while the other fumbled to free the crude weapon belted to his hip. Determined to have a weapon that wouldn't betray him, Marcus had fashioned, a primeval axe made from a sheared tongue of slate wedged and bound in place to a tree bough.

We heard the splintery crash-thump of the logs striking the bottom of the slope – where we'd strewn jagged rocks as big as beer kegs to ensure an unpleasant end to Ninurta's little trip.

"Let's finish this," he snarled wetly, baring his teeth in a red grin. "Together."

With blood smeared across his skin in dark splotches, hefting his slate bladed axe, he looked like a frenzied warrior from the dawn of man.

"Together!" The fire in his eyes was infectious. My wings opened and swung forward, feather-like tines of steel – both sword and shield – responding to my every whim.

We were halfway to the cusp of the hill when Ninurta sprang, fleet as a stag, to the top of the slope.

"A valiant attempt," he said mildly before letting the snapped noose slip from his fingers. He brushed snow from his coat. "But I am afraid it's not good enough."

"I'm just getting warmed up." I snarled the lie and almost believed it as I launched forward. Marcus, clutching his stone axe in both hands, prowled to my left looking for an opening. We'd planned this attack formation as a hail Mary. I hoped we lived long enough to see if it worked.

Two wings, one high, one low, lanced out, razored pinions ready to slice him into three pieces. The metal creations responded naturally, flowing as quickly as my mind could think. The first two strikes were almost spoiled by my shock at their alacrity.

Ninurta's agility spared him my first assault. He danced backward, slipping away by scant centimetres. I followed him, alternating probing stabs with two wings while the other two remained bent to guard me against attack.

But no attack came.

He sprang and slid along the crest of the slope, his feet somehow never running afoul on the slick, snowy ground. I went after him, wings lashing up, down, and across. Marcus jogged alongside us like a dog hoping for scraps. My feet hit a frost slicked undulation in the ground, and in trying to stay upright I sent a slash so wide that Marcus had to duck beneath my wing stroke.

"Careful," Ninurta taunted with a rich, rolling laugh. "This dance is not for the clumsy."

My breath billowed out in gasps of steam. I looked at Ninurta and saw his chest rise and fall in a steady rhythm, his breath gentle, vanishing puffs in the cold night air.

"Dance with this!" I lunged at him with all four wings arched forward.

The topmost two shot over his shoulders as he sank down just enough to avoid them creasing his suit. The lower two stopped dead when his hands clamped over the seeking blades. I felt the terrible strength of his will as much as the power of his muscles.

I tried to drive the blade plumes upward with body and mind, but nothing happened. Then, as I tried to twist the wayward upper wings for another attack, I felt his powers pushing back. Like a swallow in a windstorm, my wings flew backward. My back arched as I threw my abilities into holding them in place, even as Ninurta's powers twisted them behind my back. I screamed in defiance, but he only smiled that deep-sea predator's grin.

Just when I thought my mind, body, or possibly both, were about to snap in Ninurta's psychic grip Marcus darted forward, coming in low and hard to slam the jagged edge of his axe into the back of Ninurta's knee.

The self-styled king of kings fell to one knee in front of me, his dark eyes wide open at the temerity of the blow. The pressure on me dropped markedly.

"Dance time's over," Marcus roared, twisting the axe free and raising it to hack at the back of the giant's skull. Ninurta slipped away from the stroke with his trademark agility, twisting as he did so to cock back a hand as Marcus' momentum carried him forward.

Marcus saw the counterattack coming and threw himself backward hard enough that the blow missed him. He sailed through the air to crash and roll back, kicking up lumps of churned snow.

Dark eyes blazing, Ninurta lunged after Marcus. His huge fist pounded the earth with a thump like a mallet. Marcus kept rolling. staying just ahead of Ninurta's furious pummelling strokes; but he had seconds before he was out-manoeuvred and flattened or driven over the edge of the slope to the rocks below.

I managed to free one wing. Fighting the oppressive power of his omnipresent metallic awareness, I could only achieve a wide slap at the demi-god. But the wings were made from industrial-grade steel, acquired from the shed's roof. Being battered by one was like taking a series of frying pan blows in rapid succession.

Ninurta rocked back at my ringing strikes but somehow held his feet. Impacts that would have fractured another man's face hadn't even left a mark.

A growing sense of desperation had me ripping another wing free, and this time my anger hammered it into a lethal thrust toward his chest.

The rage driven stab ripped through the tailored suit like tissue paper, driving toward flesh. I'd expected resistance, the constriction of meat clinging to the impaling blade, but instead I heard a sharp clang. The thrusting wing slid off Ninurta's chest and along his ribs to the squeal of metal grating on metal.

Folds of shorn fabric fell away to reveal unmarked flesh.

My stomach retreated toward the soles of my feet as I took another swipe at him. This time, looking me right in the eye, he raised an open hand. Blades that should have sliced his arm off instead sent up a burst of sparks as they bounced off his open palm, utterly impotent.

"I seem to have misjudged you, my child," he said. "If this is the best you can manage, I vastly over-estimated your abilities."

"You talk too much," Marcus barked as he renewed his attack.

He feigned a swing at Ninurta's legs and then hewed down on the demigod's shoulder like a lumberjack splitting a log. The force of the blow required Ninurta to shuffle slightly to the side, but the blow had little effect.

Marcus pressed in, desperate to knock Ninurta off his feet. Blow after crushing blow struck against Ninurta's shoulder, arm, and back, but he did not fall.

"You are becoming tiresome." Ninurta grabbed Marcus by the front of his shirt and tossed him toward the shed.

Marcus flew, landed hard and rolled across the snow, coming to a stop just outside of a yawning bay door. He was slow to rise.

"Surrendering at this point could spare you and your pet no small amount of pain," Ninurta suggested in that annoyingly unruffled tone.

I took a deep breath and let out a growl. Ambush and brute force hadn't worked; what did I have left?

My metallic sense buzzed with strange tones and swirling auras that I wouldn't expect out here. It was more than just the helicopter, the auras resonated as though within reach.

Raising all four wings to shield myself, I reached out with my metallic sense and nearly recoiled as my mind touched Ninurta.

His body seethed with off-key metallic songs, constantly circulating streams of metal in tune with his every movement. He was so suffused with various elements I wasn't sure there was any difference between living flesh and living metal. It was awe-inspiring and terrifying in equal measure.

My mind felt a pulse of Ninurta's will at the same time I heard a dark chuckle.

"Do you understand now?" He squared his shoulders and opened his arms as though welcoming the next attack. "Do you have any idea?"

"I have one."

I threw out my ringed hand, punching not against his body but into the metallic auras with my mind. I gathered them in my mental fist like the strings of a cello and drew them out. It was like wrestling a cyclone out of the sky, but with the rings feeding into my own power, the streams warped and flexed my direction.

I heard a sharp, pained intake of breath.

"What are you doing?"

Ninurta's roar snapped my eyes open and what I saw startled me so much I nearly lost my grip.

Thin wisps of red steam rose from the demigod's skin, tiny motes reflecting the moonlight in flashes. The wisps formed thin contrails lazily snaking their way toward me. Staring in amazement at the success of my gambit, I caught a glimpse of Ninurta's face. Something alien came into his features: fear. For the first time in a very long time, Ninurta, king of mad kings, was scared.

The expression was quickly buried under an avalanche of rage. His glare threatened to light me ablaze, as I felt his power surge outward in a hate-fuelled shockwave.

My attention divided between the metal I drew from his body and what I was seeing, that barest distraction was the chink he drove through, breaking my hold on his living metal. The bloody fog and its cargo of metal particles flew back to Ninurta to be absorbed into his flesh.

"I am no longer amused." Ninurta's voice was as hard and flat as a bar of beaten iron.

The rage simmering in his eyes filled me with dread as he stalked forward. I needed to move, but terror numbed my mind and slowed my limbs.

Ninurta didn't wait for me to pull myself together.

Like a tidal wave his power crashed down on me, folding my wings around me with such force I was knocked flat. The cold slap of snow against the back of my neck broke my shock just as the wings began to contract, razored pinions cutting into my clothes and flesh. With a mental heave I shoved outward, holding them at bay as I fought for control.

The wings twisted around each other in our competing grips, growing more and more mangled. I drew deeply on the power of the rings again and managed to break his hold. Drawing the remains of the wings together like a huge knotted bludgeon, I launched it at Ninurta.

The gnarled metal club spun end over end and I drove it on with all I had until it struck Ninurta full in the chest. Demigod and missile sailed through the air to smash into the helicopter. The side of the aircraft buckled around Ninurta, shards of glass and metal flying, pinning him inside.

He wasn't beaten, but the fight was over. Cuts from the wings leaked blood over my torn clothes. Pain worked with exhaustion to drain me completely and I struggled to find the strength to climb to my feet.

I looked at Marcus, limping toward me, one of his legs stiff and dragging. He nodded, his battered face fighting to give me an encouraging smile. He was waiting on me, patiently like always.

Ninurta emerged from the ruined aircraft and I felt his anger sizzle through the air like heat rippling off a furnace. He rose not just out of the wreckage but into the air to glare down at us.

Marcus spat and made a staggering throw with his axe, the lopsided missile sailed off into the dark, missing its target.

Ninurta floated toward us, seeming to savour the dread inspired by his slow, sinister approach.

We'd fought hard, but we could still buy more time.

"Let's go," I said.

Marcus and I made a lurching retreat back into the utility shed.

Ninurta didn't stop us. I threw out a lash of power to drag the bay door shut behind us, plunging our world into darkness. Hand in hand we picked our way toward the rear of the shed.

"So this is how you would die then?" Ninurta's disdain was clear even through the closed door. "Cowering like cornered vermin? You are utterly unworthy of the gifts of my blood!"

"Keep waggin', gaffer," Marcus said. "Just keep waggin' that tongue."

"I could crush you like a parasite picked from a beast's back."

There was a squeal of tortured metal as the walls of the shed buckled inwards. Toolboxes shuddered and jangled, and the two vehicles bounced and skidded towards each other just as Marcus and I passed between them. We sprang clear as they crashed together.

"Or perhaps I could sear you off like a leech."

The walls stopped collapsing, which was just as well because the escape hatch we'd fashioned in the back of the shed had been reduced to a narrow slit. I felt a change in the metal as the walls began to shimmer and glow. My skin prickled as a wave of heat washed over me.

"Wait," I urged Marcus, too late.

A searing hiss was followed by a choked back cry of pain, his attempt to open the hatch thwarted.

The glow of the walls grew as the heat intensified as Marcus stuffed his burned fingers into his mouth, no doubt to cool them as well as muffle any further cries of pain. The room continued to brighten as the temperature rose, making it hard to breathe.

My vision began to blur, spots springing up in my field of vision as I tried to gather the focus it would take to open the hatch with my powers. My heart hammered in my ears as I gasped, the air seeming terribly thin.

Marcus crumpled next to me, and I realised with a drowsy blink that I was on my knees on the dirt floor. I smelled smoke and realised with a level of calm that was entirely inappropriate that the smoke was coming from me: wisps rose from my clothes, my skin, and the ends of my hair.

"Or perhaps something more dramatic." Ninurta's voice came from somewhere far off.

The temperature dropped as the glow receded from the walls.

"Yes, perhaps I should introduce you and these hallowed witnesses to the power that brought the proud kings of Mesopotamia to their knees. Listen now to your coming death, and despair. Don't worry; I'll give you plenty of time."

The portal was fading from sight as I fought for consciousness. My limbs felt as heavy as lead weights.

Somewhere high, high above the shed, I heard a strange sound.

"Now you will come to understand the power you so foolishly scorned!" Ninurta bellowed as the sound grew.

"Give it a rest," I said, beginning to sink down on top of Marcus.

He wasn't holding me, but touching him was good enough. Here at the end.

A rush of cold, clean air slapped my face and punched its way into my shrivelled lungs. I found the strength to lift my head and see that the hatch had been opened. Moonlight sparkled on a pool of melted snow. It was beautiful.

A figure, nothing more than a silhouette, passed through the portal. Outside, the strange sound was growing.

"Get up," hissed a voice. My oxygen-starved brain struggled to remember it, I'd heard it before.

Hands gripped me, dragging me to my feet.

"Ibby please!" the voice begged.

With a groan I compelled my muscles into service.

I staggered a few steps through the open portal. Looking up at the now open sky, a star streaked through the heavens. Ninurta's words bubbled up in my mind: it was coming straight toward us.

I swung around drunkenly, almost keeling over in the mud.

"Marcus!" I croaked through a desiccated throat.

A woman emerged from the hatch dragging Marcus by the arm.

Stumbling over my own feet, I went to help her. Together we yanked Marcus through the hatch and into the frigid mud. The cold and wet impact startled Marcus into a coughing wakefulness. We each got under an arm and started an ungainly run into the woods behind the shed.

The winter air stung my lungs but cleared my head. I looked over at our rescuer in the dapples of moonlight between the tree branches.

Daria looked back at me, eyes wide with fear. "Run! Don't talk!"

I looked back just as we dropped down into a small valley – to see the falling star strike the shed behind us.

Trees groaned and bent as a ripping wind tore at their tops and the world erupted in fire.

# FOURTEEN

We ran through burning trees, Marcus somehow getting his legs under him, which was good because the man was ridiculously heavy.

Snow hissed into churning clouds of steam. The world was wreathed in a cold fog that clung to the skin like slime. The fog mixed with ash and smoke to smother and choke. My head swam with the madness of the situation, but there was no time to figure it out.

So I ran.

My foot caught on a root and I pitched forward, sliding across the ground. At least there was no pain. I was too numb for that. Wheezing, I tried to force air into my lungs, utterly convinced that I had nothing left. Looking up, I saw Marcus and Daria staggering back to get me.

Marcus's features were stamped with exhaustion and Daria hunched over, eyes darting everywhere, as though terrified Ninurta might appear from any direction. I drove my fists down as I fought to rise.

"Nearly there." Daria slipped a hand under my arm and helped me up.

I found my feet again, moving shoulder to shoulder across a speckled, snowy landscape scattered with trees. I wanted to ask *where* we nearly were but couldn't find the energy for words.

We continued to run until the trees began to spread and we found ourselves trudging through snow in an open field that sloped gently downward. I sobbed a cry of thankfulness, fighting to keep my legs from collapsing. At the bottom of the slope, a military type Land Rover sat with its engine growling softly.

"Come on!" Daria called, plunging through the snow toward the vehicle.

I slowed to an inching stagger.

"Who is she?" Marcus asked, seeming all too happy to adopt my slower pace.

Daria reached the vehicle and turned to beckon us on before throwing open the driver's door.

"She was a friend, once." I slid over to give Marcus what little support my shoulder could offer.

"Can we trust her?"

Marcus gasped a curse as he came down on his damaged leg.

"I don't know."

I looked back to the horizon of burning trees.

"I'm not sure we have a choice. She at least seems determined to get us out of here."

"I'll take it."

We reached the Land Rover and I helped Marcus climb into the tarp draped bed. We were breathless by the time we were settled against the back of the bed.

Daria appeared at the tailgate and gave us a once over.

"Both need medical attention," she declared, presumably into a communication device, her tone clipped and frustrated. "There's no time. Need to make distance."

She slammed the tailgate shut, then climbed into the driver's seat.

The idling motor roared to life.

My mind told me to be wary: stay alert, remember what Daria is, remember what she had done.

My body decided it needed sleep more. Within minutes I was dozing, curled up next to Marcus and rocked into blessed oblivion by the bouncing gait of the vehicle.

---

I AWOKE ON THE GROUND, naked from the waist up, with a glaring light sweeping from my face down over my body and back again. Everything else was darkness.

I tried to twist my body away from the revealing light, but I only managed a fitful twitch before I collapsed back onto the ground.

"Hold still," Daria's voice instructed from behind the light. "After I've cleaned the wounds and bandaged them, you can move."

Her matter of fact direction irked me to a degree far beyond what her words merited, but I found I couldn't even will my mouth to open and curse her.

I felt her working on my body, swabbing the lacerations from my crushed wings, but it was an awareness of pressure and changes in temperature. There was no pain, which was a discomfort of its own.

I lay there, completely helpless, as she wrapped my wounds and applied salve to the burns on my neck, face, and hands. The vulnerability ate at me.

Daria nodded once she had completed her ministrations and I felt something cold and sharp slide free from my neck. As the intrusion into my body withdrew, I was reminded of another such a violation by an edimmu.

In control of my body once more, I rolled away from her, knocking the cast-off medical supplies in every direction. I climbed to my feet clumsily, one hand cocked back in a fist while the other was held out with a warding palm. My metallic sense swept around for anything I might use as a weapon.

"Ibby, wait." Daria rose from her crouch, her headlamp stabbing into my eyes. She put out a hand. "It's alright. Calm down."

Several steel chains were close at hand, the Land Rover a few feet to my left. I drew the snarled chains up, setting their links to clinking as they swung menacingly around me. The bandages around my chest made it hard to draw a full breath, but I sucked in enough air to loose a warning through bared teeth.

"How dare you!" I spat. "You pumped your poison through me!"

Daria was a vague silhouette, but her hands rose palms up in surrender.

"I'm sorry." She slid back as the chains rattled like Jacob Marley's. "I wanted to make sure you wouldn't hurt yourself when you came to."

"What are these for then?" I demanded, shaking the chains as they orbited me. "If the poison didn't work, were you going to chain me up like an animal?"

Daria stared before responding in a flat, dry tone.

"Those are the snow chains for the Land Rover, and I think it would be incredibly stupid to try and bind an Inconquo with metal chains, don't you?"

Allowing the chains to sink to the floor, I had enough sense to feel sheepish, though I still held the links in my mental grip. Looking around I saw nothing but darkness except where Daria's lamp revealed a bare and grungy expanse of concrete. Gooseflesh crept along my arms and threatened to engulf the rest of me.

"Where are we?"

"An abandoned garage near Raylees," Daria answered. "I've got a plane chartered from Eshott Airfield in a couple of hours, but the roads were getting treacherous and I needed to check your injuries. I still need to look at Marcus' leg."

It all made sense, but the memory of everything Daria had put us through, combined with what Ninurta had told me, left me more than a little suspicious.

"How do you know who Marcus is?"

Daria let out a small sigh before answering, her voice strained with forced patience.

"He told me. He was awake when we got here and insisted I look after you first. He wanted to watch over you but he fell asleep." She cocked her head toward the Land Rover.

I flinched a little as she crouched, then felt silly when she stood with a dangling lump of fabric.

"You should get dressed." She held out my clothes. "We need to get you clean ones, but they'll at least keep you warm until we're in the air."

I dressed as Daria moved to the back of the Land Rover.

"Why is it so dark?"

"The garage gets used as a flophouse from time to time," Daria explained as she climbed into the bed of the vehicle. "So they blacked out the windows. Can't have nosey people peeping in on their recreational activities."

My shoe scuffed against something that gave a brittle crunch, and I cringed, hoping I wasn't scooting around spent hypodermics.

"Charming."

I watched her do a quick inspection of Marcus's twisted leg before drawing out a pair of bandage scissors.

"It's clear." She began cutting up the length of the injured leg's trouser. "I wouldn't walk around barefoot, but I think I cleaned out the space around the Land Rover well enough."

To my amazement, Marcus didn't stir as she slit the garment all the way to his grey underpants. Quick and precise, she yanked the liberated fabric away, revealing his muscled leg. His knee was swollen and the colour of a plum – all that strength hadn't spared him serious injury.

I swallowed a sob as Daria tentatively probed the distended purple skin that seemed ready to split open. Marcus shuddered and let out a low moan at the touch, but didn't wake up.

"Running on the leg didn't do him any favours, but I don't think there is a fracture."

Daria did something at her waist before I heard the clink of a belt buckle and she shifted toward Marcus's face. She shook his shoulder, and when he didn't respond slapped lightly at his cheek until his eyes fluttered open.

"Huh? What?" he muttered thickly, squinting up at the light.

"Open your mouth."

"What f-uph," was all he managed before she stuffed the folded strap of her belt into his mouth.

Daria moved towards his knee with a relentless insistence. I saw what was coming just before her hands braced his knee on either side.

"Bite down hard!"

Her hands went into action and there was a wet, almost wooden, pop.

Marcus's entire body arched in agony, his teeth clamping down on the leather that muffled his scream. His hands knotted into trembling fists to pound against the bed, while his head beat a staccato tattoo. His uninjured leg thrashed, nearly knocking me out of the Land Rover as I crawled toward him. Daria had secured the injured leg between her own and was wrapping it in a long, swaddling bandage.

"Marcus, I'm here." I slid up next to him, a soothing hand on his arm.

His breath billowed in my face, and I could hear the jingling buckle of the belt still clutched in his teeth. I reached out to stroke his brow. His skin was cold and clammy, but I could feel his entire body clenched with pain. My throat threatened to close up, seeing him like this.

"He'll need an X-Ray and an MRI, but it'll do for now," Daria said as she extricated herself from Marcus and exited the vehicle.

"I'm here," I whispered, tears rolling down my cheeks.

Marcus collapsed against the bed of the Land Rover. His breathing was rapid but steady, and I felt his pounding heart slow when I laid a hand against his chest.

The snow chains rattled and clinked as Daria fixed them to the tyres. For a second, I considered helping her. But when Marcus reached out and gripped the hand I'd placed over his chest, I couldn't leave him.

As Daria was finishing the last tyre he whispered hoarsely, "That went better than I expected."

"What were you expecting?" I almost laughed. "For her to amputate?"

Marcus did laugh, but the sound was soon swallowed by another fit of coughing.

"I wasn't talking about my leg," he croaked after the fit subsided. "I meant the fight with Ninurta."

The bemused smile fell from my face at the first Inconquo's name. Images of the night flicked through my mind like a video recording. If this was his idea of cheering me up, it wasn't working.

"What did you think was going to happen?"

"I thought we'd be dead, obviously."

"Ah. Well, we've bought a little time." I was unable to keep the bleakness out of my tone. "Nothing more."

"Wasn't that the point?" He chuckled dryly and cleared his throat. "Mission accomplished *and* we're not dead."

It was hard to argue with that logic. I smiled at him. His hand squeezed mine gently before sliding up to stroke my cheek. My skin was raw, but he was so gentle I felt nothing but a cool tingle at the caress.

Daria slid into the driver's seat, turned on the vehicle and pulled us out of the garage. Leaving the engine to idle, she got out and closed the door before settling in behind the wheel again.

"We need to make good time," she called as she revved the engine. "Sorry in advance for how rough this could get."

I tore my eyes away from Marcus's ashen face, blinking in the light. "You still have a lot of explaining to do."

Daria didn't look back, but I could feel the razor smile in her answer. "More than you know, luv, more than you know."

# FIFTEEN

The next twenty-four hours were a blur of planes, trains and automobiles. We landed in the south, in rain rather than snow, and had a chance to clean up before boarding a train to London. We sat across from one another at a table while Daria brought us up to speed, rain lashing at the windows as the train ate up the miles.

"Once Ninurta bent me to his service, I was forced to play the long game. Part of that meant cooperating with Winterthür when it was time for him to wake up." Daria sighed and looked out the window at the green smudge of the countryside.

Marcus and I shared a look but neither of us responded. I thought I knew what he was wondering. Daria had saved us, but did that mean she could be trusted?

"I'm sorry it is all so cloak-and-dagger," Daria went on, folding her hands on the table-top, "but please understand that I've *never* shared this with anyone."

"Oh, yes," I sniped. "It would be difficult to share that you've been working for a mass-murdering madman for thousands of years, and had to join an evil secret society to set him free." My hard words were followed by a heavy silence before I added in a softer tone, "Jackie might never walk again because of how you played your long game."

"You have every right to be angry." Daria did not look away, accepting my anger and harsh words calmly, her voice full of regret. "I am not asking for forgiveness, no matter how much I would wish for it. I just want you to understand, to know what has happened, *what is happening*, and why."

I looked out the window, working to move my ire about Jackie into the background so I could listen. Daria waited for me to give her permission to proceed, studying me intently while I watched the muddied countryside roll by. The dismal vista did nothing to improve my mood.

I took a deep breath as Marcus took my hand. "Go ahead. Tell us everything."

Daria seemed to relax, letting her hands slip off the table and leaning back. "It would take me days to tell my story, and we don't have that kind of time. What you need to know is this: Ninurta made me the keeper of his resting place, but I've never willingly served him. My phylactery was held hostage with him, and to get it back I needed to do my part."

"That's where I'm not clear," Marcus interjected. "I'm new to all this, but if I understand how that phylactery thing works, wouldn't it being with Ninurta, in his un-openable tomb, be a good thing for you? You'd never have to worry about anyone else finding it, and if Ninurta was sleeping he couldn't use it against you. Win-win, right?"

Daria nodded but gave him the saddest smile I'd ever seen.

"Yes, if I had wanted to live this long. But even before I met Ninurta, I hated what I'd become. I didn't, don't, want to live forever. You can probably imagine how ... uncomfortable these past few millennia have been."

The confession cut through the layers of anger and disgust, even banishing the image of paralysed Jackie for a moment. Daria, a woman who'd saved my life multiple times and who I'd once counted a friend, wanted to die.

I looked at her, realising, not for the first time, that I barely understood this striking creature who'd crept into my life. Suspicion, empathy, and anger fought a three-way tug of war as I watched her wrestle to putting words to the burden she'd borne since before the great pyramids of Giza had been built.

"What about the attack on Museum Station?" I asked. "The attack that nearly destroyed Lowe, and left Jackie paralysed."

"Herr Niemand found my phylactery when they opened Ninurta's tomb. That was a possibility I hadn't considered. The Group of Winterthür wanted Kezsarak's cube back and held my phylactery hostage to ensure I would assist them to get it. I'm sorry about Jackie. That wasn't part of my plan. I didn't realise what Sark had done – I thought your group had the cube."

"Then why are you helping us now?"

"I have retrieved my phylactery. Neither Ninurta nor the Group of Winterthür have any hold over me. I wish to fulfil my mission for Lamashtu: destroy Ninurta. Whatever the cost."

"Why now?" I asked. "Why is *this* the time to end it all?"

"The short answer is you," she said with a fractional shrug. "You are the first person I've met in my long, long life who stands a chance of defeating him."

The answer hit me like a sled between the eyes. My cheeks burned as shame flooded me. "You've over-estimated me by f-"

"No." Daria's sharp word cut me off. "I haven't."

Her gaze burned into mine, glimmering with inhuman intensity. The weight of that look settled heavily over my shoulders, along with the weight of expectation.

"It wasn't even a fight, Daria." I shook my head, memories of the recent battle flashing through my mind. "He toyed with us."

Marcus shifted and cleared his throat, looking down at me. "Not to be grotesquely optimistic, but after Ninurta pitched me like a ragdoll, I saw you do... something... to him. It looked like you were pulling something out of him. Even with my bells rung, I could see that you were turning the tables. He was *scared*, Ibby."

Daria's eyes darted back and forth between us, widening. "What happened?"

The hope in her voice, so urgent and bright, made my gut feel full of ash.

"I tried to draw out the metal that's within in him, that's part of him," I explained. "But even catching him off guard and using all the power in the rings, he still beat me down like I was an afterthought. I just wasn't strong enough."

For several heartbeats, no one spoke. The thrumming of the train and the occasional murmur of conversation from further up the compartment were the only sounds.

"No offence to Marcus," Daria said, eyes still shining with hope, "but you faced Ninurta nearly on your own. We can change that. I can change that."

I swung my gaze back to Daria, narrowing my eyes. "You didn't seem to be so eager for a fight back in Northumberland."

"You were spent and injured by the time I got there," Daria replied. "I may want to die, but that doesn't mean that I want to waste my death."

We lapsed into silence as the countryside gave way to the suburban expanse that girdled London. I felt Daria waiting. Not waiting for me to forgive her, but waiting for some sign that I was willing to work with her again. Which meant I had to trust her, believe her story. I didn't want to. My love for and allegiance to Jackie made me want to throw her offer back in her face and leave her as soon as we pulled into the train station. But though I hadn't given her any indication yet, I *did* believe her. Marcus and I were alive thanks to her. Not only that, we needed an ally that did not rely on metal weapons in order to fight Ninurta.

I looked over at Marcus and in his look was a silent communication. He believed her story too and he was all for working with her.

Finally, I cleared my throat and Daria straightened at the sound, those dark and expectant eyes on mine.

"I guess you've got a plan?"

A sly smile spread across her face.

"I thought you'd never ask. You aren't going to like it, but it is our best chance at saving the bloody world, so let's not muck it up. Get me in front of Jody Marks. I'll only lay it out once."

# SIXTEEN

At the train station in London, I left Daria and Marcus sitting on a bench while I found a pharmacy and bought Marcus a set of crutches. Then we used the tube to make our way to the TNC offices. We left Daria in a coffee shop while Marcus and I went to talk to Marks about her idea. The moment we stepped into the lobby of The Nakesh Corporation building, something felt wrong.

Everything had the same polished, nothing-to-see-here normalcy, but there was a brittle tension in the air.

"I know Daria is waiting for us, but shall we check on Uncle Iry and Jackie before we find Marks?" I asked Marcus as we crossed the lobby.

He nodded. "Funny. I was just thinking the same thing."

Anxiety wound its way around my spine like a climbing vine as I used my ID card to board the elevator. As we glided down floor after floor, I told myself the unease was only in my mind.

"Lobby was painted a different colour," Marcus said. "Different panelling around the elevator."

I looked up at him with surprise. "So you're into interior decorating, along with weightlifting and dangerous women?"

Marcus snorted and shook his head. "Not so much, but while my dangerous woman was running around chasing bad guys, I was stuck in this building with nothing but time. People watching in the lobby was a distraction between push-ups and worrying."

While I felt a pang of sympathy for the trials Marcus had endured, the changes to the lobby struck me as too timely to be coincidental.

"What do you think happened?"

Marcus tapped the ends of his crutches on the floor thoughtfully.

"Not sure. But there were four security officers in the lobby."

"How many are there usually?" I asked.

"One."

I let out a slow breath and fought the urge to use my powers increase the elevator's speed. I needed to see Jackie and Uncle Iry. I needed to know they were okay. My heart had buggered off to rent a room in my throat and seemed determined to stay there for every agonising second it took to descend to the hospital floors.

When the doors finally parted, we found ourselves blocked by Bordeaux, armed and armoured for the battlefield. The sight of his openly carried combat rifle filled my stomach with ice.

"What's happened? Where's Jackie? Where's my uncle?"

Bordeaux held up a hand, whether to calm me or slow me down, I wasn't sure; but his usually robotic demeanour faltered.

"Ms Davies is in her room, just as you left her. She was unharmed by the attack, though I imagine the stress didn't help her condition, but I'm no—"

Stone cold, brutally honest Bordeaux was stalling.

"And my uncle?" I cut him off mid-blather.

Bordeaux paled, his voice raw. "They took him."

I staggered as the strength went out of my legs. Marcus put an arm around my waist to brace me as I wheezed, laying a hand against my chest. I felt as though my heart was being crushed in a vice.

"The Group of Winterthür took your uncle."

---

THE FRUSTRATION, sorrow, and shame burning in Jackie's eyes when I entered her room stole what little heart I had to speak.

I trudged over to her and plopped down in the seat next to her. Unshed tears brimmed in my eyes, but anger beyond expression simmered in my blood. My hands knotted into quivering fists and ground against the top of my thighs. I'd gone immediately to Marks' office, spewing accusations, tears pouring down my face. She'd been insufferably calm while she'd explained how the building had been infiltrated. A trusted courier had died, their ID and delivery schedule taken. Recently hired security guards had been duped, the period of their probation giving Winterthür an opportunity to take advantage of a vulnerable moment. Marks had apologized. Told me TNC took every precaution but was not impervious. No intelligence agency was. All in all we should be thankful that the loss of life hadn't been higher. She promised me we'd get my uncle back, but who was she to make such promises?

I felt Jackie's eyes on me, knew she wanted to be helpful and encouraging, but she seemed to be having the same trouble I was. Impotent rage did anything but loosen the tongue.

By the time Jackie spoke, I was so lost in strangled thoughts that I started at the sound of her voice.

"They told you how it happened?"

I nodded as I stared into the middle distance, unable to bear looking her in the eyes.

"It happened so fast. Suddenly, they were in the halls searching rooms." Jackie raked a hand through her hair. "I tried to get Iry to hide, to sneak out, to ... to ..."

Her voice broke, a rasping sob rocking her body and drawing my gaze at last.

"To do anything except watch over a bed-bound cripple." She ground her teeth and beat her useless, blanket-swathed legs. "Damn it all, he wouldn't leave *me*. He was trying to protect me!"

I reached out to take her hands as the fists became claws, raking at the blankets and her legs.

"Jackie!" Sweat beaded my forehead as I struggled to stop her. "Jackie, please!"

Her screeching shrivelled into a bitter whimper as she finally allowed me move her hands to her sides. The blankets were in disarray, leaving her exposed. Angry welts crisscrossed her thighs. I straightened the covers over her as I fought down more tears, then I bent over and hugged her.

"I'm sorry," she moaned, her head falling against my shoulder. "I'm so sorry, Ibby! I was useless; I am useless."

Jackie's final despairing declaration knocked out the last of my self-pity. Ninurta had beaten me, Iry was gone, and none of that changed the fact that she needed me. Soon, I feared a whole lot more people would need me.

"Jackie, stop." I took her face in my hands and looked at her, rubbing away a tear with the pad of my thumb. "You. Are. Not. Useless."

Jackie's face was blotched with red patches and wet from weeping. Though she couldn't speak between hitching breaths, she gave a shake of denial.

"You are not useless," I whispered, keeping her face turned towards me and my eyes locked on hers. "You are my best friend and the strongest woman I know, and I need you. I need your help."

Jackie sniffled, her breathing catching at each inhalation, but her expression changed from broken surrender to bewilderment. “What?”

“I need you to help me fight Ninurta.” I released her face and sat on the side of her bed.

She blinked and brushed away another tear. “How the bloody hell do you expect me to do that?”

She gestured toward her limp legs in a quick angry sweep, that had me tensing to restrain her again.

“I need your mind, not your body.” I replied, drawing my feet up and perching my heels on the edge of the mattress. “I need your experience and knowledge more than I need your fists or feet.”

She studied my face. “What do you mean?”

I took her hand. “I need your way of thinking; your self-defence training. You told me that one of the things they drilled into you during your fighting classes is that you should assume your enemy is bigger, stronger, and more dangerous than you. Well, Ninurta is bigger, stronger than me, and so much more dangerous. I need to learn to take on someone like that.”

Jackie frowned, her eyes expressing a world of doubts.

“Just because I took self-defence doesn’t make me a soldier. I don’t know strategy.”

“That’s just it,” I pressed, “I’m not looking for a military perspective. I need a cage-fighting, go-down-swinging mindset. That’s what you can give me.”

And what I could give her was a distraction from her agony over Uncle Iry in the meantime.

Jackie's frown deepened, but she swiped away the last of her tears.

"When you are fighting someone who has you beat at almost every level..." Her eyes went soft as her mind sifted through her rolodex of fighting knowledge. "You do everything you can to get away. You create space, give yourself room to manoeuvre, and the second you can, you run like your hair is on fire."

I waited as her thoughts came together, knowing she wasn't finished.

"But sometimes there's no way out." An angry light kindled in her doe eyes. "And if that's the case, the next thing is maximum damage."

Her gaze swung to me, focused again.

"You bring the pain." Cords of muscle stood out on her neck. "It becomes your mission to hit them in every place, in every way that will do damage. But more than that, you show them that to keep them from getting what they want, you aren't afraid to die."

I hadn't expected to survive Ninurta's first attack so I was already on board with that.

"We learned how to strike at sensitive places, not just because pain can slow your attacker down, but because pain makes people angry and afraid. And angry, fearful people are stupid. Pain is the mortar, injury the bricks. So there is only one question then ..."

I nodded. "How do you hurt a demigod?"

---

I GAVE myself a cooling off period of an hour before approaching Marks again, wishing I could take a day. I went to the cafeteria on Jackie's floor and got a cup of coffee, pacing among the tables and talking my heart into a normal rhythm. I didn't have time to sleep on things. Daria was waiting, and I'd been too shattered by losing Iry to have broached the subject with Marks yet.

When I finished the coffee I went back up to Marks' office and knocked on her door, letting her know this time I was ready to be civil.

There was the sound of a phone settling back into its cradle and then, "Come."

Pushing through her door, I crossed to the chair across from her. She eyed me, leaning back in her chair.

"Back so soon?"

"In the heat of my last visit," I began, taking a breath and resting my hands on the arms of the chair, "I forgot to tell you about Daria."

"Daria..." Marks canted her head to the side and a line appeared between her brows.

"Daria is an edimmu."

I was about to explain what an edimmu was when Marks' expression shifted. She paled and grew serious. She already knew.

"What have you gotten yourself involved with, Ibukun Bashir?" she asked quietly.

I cleared my throat, assuming that question was rhetorical. "Daria wants to die, but before she does, she wants to fulfil her promise to her master, Lamashtu."

"What promise is that?" Marks leaned forward ever so slightly, her fine brows arching.

"Taking out Ninurta."

Her expression fell. "Edimmu are frightening, but if you've described Ninurta accurately, even she cannot withstand him."

"That's why she's proposing we work together."

Marks listened quietly while I relayed how the edimmu had rescued Marcus and I, and Daria's desire to meet her and discuss a plan. Marks' response was to ask me to leave the room for five minutes while she made a phone call.

When she called me back into her office, her demeanour had changed from wary to settled. Whoever she had called, my guess was it was to a superior, they'd given her some kind of certainty.

"I agree to meet with her."

Lowering myself back into the chair, I cocked an eyebrow. "That was easy."

Marks shrugged. "Allegiances pass from one hand to another in this business all the time. Even if you weren't vouching for Daria, I would at least listen to what she had to offer."

I shifted uncomfortably. "I'm not clear on what exactly the offer is, she said she'd present to us at the same time. She's only told me she has a plan, and information."

"I know." Marks gave me a knowing look. "But given the experience and expertise of the creature we are talking about, those two things are worth quite a bit, whatever they may be."

I nodded.

"So how do we contact her?" Marks steepled her fingers, her eyes glinting with eagerness.

"She gave me this number." I presented a folded strip of paper. "She said once she receives a call from your personal phone and you stay on the line for ten seconds after the tone she'll know you've accepted her entering the building. She'll enter the lobby, and is fine with security screening; she wants it understood that calling the number acknowledges that she is to be treated as an asset, not a threat."

Marks' eyes narrowed fractionally, then she took the paper while reaching for the phone on her desk.

"Sorry," I interjected before she could pick up the receiver. "She said your *personal* mobile."

Marks' expression flattened into a glassy semblance of her usual unflappable, slightly ironic facade.

"I suppose there's no point in asking how she would know to recognise this number," she mused as she drew a phone out of her jacket pocket.

"Should we go downstairs to meet her?" I asked, after Marks pocketed her phone, trying not to squirm under her unrelenting scrutiny.

"No, she'll be brought up after she's cleared by security, although that's a formality. The most dangerous thing about that *woman* is not what she carries on her, but in her."

Remembering Pierre Gwaffu's demonic powers, I had to agree.

"But you've worked with supernatural beings before," I said. "That's why you have Dr Emoto, right? You're used to this sort of thing."

"That may be, but supernaturals are categorized into classes. I'm accustomed to working with soldiers and elementals, leaving supernaturals outside those classes to others. Beings as ancient and dangerous as an edimmu are part of a disconcerting list. The head of our organization, Devon Nakesh, would normally work with someone like Daria, but he is not available at this time. So." She shrugged and ran a hand over her perfect updo.

I stared at my ally, a riot of feelings surging and subsiding like waves. Enigmatic and yet seeming supremely pragmatic, she was the strangest woman I had ever met, and that included Daria. I wondered what Marks had seen in her time.

"How many classes of supernatural beings have you encountered?" I asked, telling myself I was just killing time until Daria arrived.

Marks' features were so precisely set she could have been wearing a mask.

"Many," she stated with irritating simplicity, before the quiet stretched into an uncomfortable silence. "Yet, not so many that I don't feel a little ... giddy at the thought of meeting a new one."

It was hard--to the point of impossible--to imagine Marks giddy but I felt that the statement might have been one of the most honest things she'd ever said. Somehow the answer rang with a deeper truth. The glimpse of utter honesty sharpened my curiosity while giving me a little more confidence.

"Are there other supernaturals here now? In this building?"

Her answer was clipped. "You don't have the clearance for that answer."

"Okay, but I'm a supernatural myself now, and we're about to embark upon a mission to take out a powerful demigod. If you had supernaturals around that could help, one would think now would be the perfect time to introduce them, so we could include them in the plan?"

She tilted her chin down. "Don't you think I would have done that already if I could have?"

I pulled a face. "I don't know. No one ever tells me anything in this bloody place until it's the last minute."

She let out a breath. "While I cannot give you details, I can tell you that I tried to have a few of our assets reassigned from a project we're setting up for in North Africa. Our CEO would not allow it. The project there is high priority."

"A demigod with the power to affect the earth's core isn't priority?" I gaped at her. "Whatever this other project is must be galactic in nature."

I'd said it ironically but Marks just nodded.

"If the timing had been better," she said, "and that project successfully concluded, we would have been able to deploy a supernatural with abilities even Ninurta could not withstand."

"What kind of supernatural are you talking about?" My heart began to pound at her words.

"I'm not permitted to say." Marks folded her hands on the desk. "You are an Inconquo. The enemy is an Inconquo. You are the best supernatural for the job that we currently have available to us."

I wanted to ask her more about this mysterious supernatural but I knew she wouldn't say any more. From the look on her face, she'd already said too much. Instead I asked, "Don't you ever get frightened by the powers you're involved with?"

Marks' gaze slid around the room, as though looking for some spy or eavesdropper foolish enough to hide in her office. When her eyes settled back on me, I knew I'd pushed too hard.

"I am not sure this conversation is beneficial at this time," she said, whatever tiny door I'd opened closing before my eyes. "You need to focus on the task at hand. I have been doing this for a while now, I am not frightened by my job. I plan to keep doing it for a good while longer, that is assuming..."

"Yeah." I sank back into my chair, disappointed. "Assuming Ninurta doesn't wipe us all out in the next few days."

"Precisely," Marks agreed and then looked positively delighted when her phone rang again. "Yes?"

Her expression became one of wary confusion as she listened.

My skin prickled at the sight and I nudged the rings, fusing them. Had Daria already turned on us?

"No, do not let them move from that spot," Marks said sharply, her voice perfectly controlled in spite of the fearful glimmer creeping into her eyes.

I rose from my seat, straining to hear what was being said on the other end of the line. "What's going on?"

Marks raised a hand to silence me as she spoke into the phone. "No, I want every team in the complex and the surrounding area to form a perimeter, but they are not to engage. I repeat: do not engage. They could bring down the whole building."

It was a kind of agony, being ready to race into danger but having to wait for direction.

"Marks!" I growled, every muscle beginning to twitch and burn with adrenaline. My feet were ready to start running without my permission.

"I'm sending her." Marks looked up, a scowl of irritation on her features. "Lobby, now."

I headed out of her office, thankful for release from the torment of waiting, but stopped at the door.

"What's down there?"

Marks was already giving more instructions to the person on the line, but she spared me a withering look.

"Daria brought a friend," she snapped. "Now go!"

She emphasised her order by jabbing a finger toward the door, as if I didn't know where it was and wasn't already halfway through it.

I bolted for the elevator. Pacing inside the metal box did something to diminish the tremors in my stomach and knees.

What was Daria doing? If she really wanted to hurt us, why the charade? If she meant to strike at The Nakesh Corporation, walking into their lobby after telling them she was coming seemed particularly ineffective. So what was she playing at, and who was down there with her?

Prepared to walk into a potentially hostile situation, I pulled the handrail from its fixings, splitting it open and flattening it. Before the doors opened, I was sheathed in a piecemeal skin of shaped metal, the armour giving a soft groan as it flexed around my movements.

Stepping out into the hallway, a quartet of security personnel were crouched in the alcove across from me, their weapons trained down the short length of the hallway leading to the lobby. Two gave me a startled look, but they recovered quickly.

"Have ye' covered, mum," one of them said softly, as she sighted down the barrel of a submachine gun towards the lobby.

It would have been rude to tell her that her weapon was little better than a popgun in this situation, so I just nodded and moved down the hall.

The empty lobby seemed cavernous and the two figures standing by the central desk small. My heart buoyed, thankful that the companion in the hooded duffle coat could not be Ninurta. I wasn't eager to face the demigod so soon after our last encounter.

"Daria?" I called. "What's going on?"

She turned from reclining against the desk, taking in my armoured form with an approving nod.

"Bringing things together." She gestured toward the figure standing next to her. "I told you I had a plan, and that plan requires cooperation."

The figure had not turned to face me, but something about the way his shoulders gathered as he waited, with elbows on the desktop, made my stomach do familiar summersaults.

I took a few steps closer. "Why didn't you tell me about this earlier? You're making everyone nervous with these games."

Daria nodded.

"I understand, but I didn't want you to say no." She gave a helpless shrug. "Not the best way to rekindle an alliance, I know, but I'm hoping that is the last time I'll ever have to bend the truth with you. I just need you to remember what I told you about this plan."

Her companion turned around, exposing a wide smile and the molten heart throbbing in his chest. Dillon Sark looked me up and down.

"I think I like the wings better," Sark said. "Though I wonder how you'd look if you tried both."

My fists rose into guard, and I scooped up every spare piece of metal I could find in a single sweep. An assortment of decor and office supplies gathered around me like a thunderhead.

"What is *he* doing here?"

Daria stepped forward, hands up.

"Remember, Ibby." Her voice was preternaturally calm. "I said you wouldn't like it, but this is our best chance. I wasn't lying about that."

# SEVENTEEN

I'd finished packing and sat at the edge of the bed, letting Marcus vent.

"I should be going with you. You need someone to watch your back," he continued, his brow creased over downcast eyes. "Especially with Sark being there."

I couldn't argue with him. He hated being left behind, but no amount of gumption would make up for the fact that his injuries made him a liability.

He sat beside me, his weight making me tilt toward him. "I know that Marks is sending Stewart's team with you, and Daria will be there. But I'm honestly not sure which woman I trust less. You should have someone you really trust watching your back."

"Maybe," I said, wrapping my arms around my knees and leaned against his shoulder. "Or maybe this way, I can do what I have to without worrying about those with me."

Marcus looked over, stricken, and I realised how that must have sounded to him.

"I didn't mean it like that," I said quickly, reaching out a hand to reassure him. "I couldn't have faced him that night without you."

"Sure, if you say so." Marcus seemed unconvinced. "But you shouldn't kid yourself that you aren't going to be worrying about other people. You are a protector, worrying comes with the gig."

Once again, I couldn't argue. I only nodded as I rose. He got to his feet as well and I slid against him for a hug, mindful of the crutches leaning against the bed.

"I've got some great things to protect," I whispered as I nestled my head against his chest. "It helps knowing what you are fighting for."

"I--" His breathing was heavy and the words caught in his throat. I shushed him and gave a quick squeeze before pulling away.

"You'll be right here with me until I get back." I tapped a finger on my heart.

"That has to be the cheesiest thing anyone has ever said to me." He chuckled.

"You think you know how to properly say goodbye, then?"

He nodded and bent to kiss me.

"I love you, Ibukun Bashir. Come back to me."

I couldn't think of this as a one-way trip. I had to face Ninurta, had to find a way to defeat him. I had to do the impossible, not to save the world but so I could get back here, back to him.

"I love you, too, and I will."

---

"YOU'VE A PLAN THEN, LUV?" Jackie asked, her eyes locked on the ceiling over her reclined bed.

"Yep, in no small part thanks to you," I leaned forward in the chair so my elbows rested on the mattress beside her head. "And I hear that you've got a plan of sorts too."

The doctors had decreed that she spend more time flat on her back to reduce the swelling. They might then be able to do reconstructive and restorative surgery on her damaged spine. The outcomes were uncertain, and recovery would be gruelling, but that there was any hope was nothing short of a miracle.

"We both have reason to be cheerful then." She rolled her head to look me in the eye. "But your plan better be to get back here on the hop. I'm going to need someone to whine at as I relearn how to walk."

I reached out a hand to tuck a stray lock of hair behind her ear.

"Stop the apocalypse and make it home in time for rehab."

"That about covers it."

Jackie studied my face, looking for something. She eventually gave voice to her search in a fragile, plaintive voice.

"You are coming back, right?"

"You bet your bonnie, wee bum I am. I'm convinced we've got more than a good chance this time."

That was being disingenuously optimistic, but I think Jackie wanted to believe me, so she nodded stiffly.

"You beat the bully proper and then get back here in short order." A spark of her old fighting spirit shone through. "Godspeed, luv."

# EIGHTEEN

As I had told Marks, Ninurta was not interested in secrecy. He had barrelled into northern Iraq near the Zagros Mountains, set up a compound with his followers and his collected children –Inconquo descendants, like Uncle Iry, from across the globe.

Both Daria and TNC had intel on these happenings, but the information wasn't hard to come by. Many foreign eyes were watching events in the war-torn country with keen interest, and though the more fantastic elements of his story were being written off, the wider world knew that a new "insurgent" was rising in Iraq. Unfortunately for all of them, Ninurta's fantastic nature was precisely what they should be concerned with. But, in fairness, if you'd told me last year about what I was doing now, I'd have called you a loon and walked away. Now I was riding over Turkey in a cargo plane with two demons and a team of fully armed former soldiers to face this insurgent on his own turf, surrounded by his followers.

I shouted to be heard over the engines as Daria and I reviewed the plan.

"... hoping that Ninurta won't be throwing down meteors for fear of killing his own."

Sark, who'd mostly kept to himself during the planning, shook his head.

"It is foolish to think he won't sacrifice a few pawns to get rid of you." His burning, unfocused gaze met mine; it was like looking into the eyes of a person caught in the grips of a nightmare. Whatever Sark had hoped for when he'd drawn Kezsarak into himself, I very much doubted he'd gotten what he wanted.

"It's not about his humanity but his pragmatism," Daria yelled back. "He'll need to draw on as many of his bloodline as possible to make his plan work. If he starts killing his strongest, he'll risk not having enough juice to pull it off."

Sark shrugged and leaned back in his seat, his expression unconvinced, but he didn't seem interested in further argument.

"You two approach the compound from the other side."

Now it was Daria's turn to be sceptical.

"It's a mistake to split our deployment. Even if Ninurta isn't throwing meteors at you, he's lethal. This could go poorly very quickly."

I shook my head, gesturing at myself with both hands. "I need him focused on me. If he spots you, it'll alert him that we're up to something."

Daria frowned and leaned forward in her safety harness. "The plan doesn't work at all if you're dead."

I laughed in a way that I hoped hid my fear. "Your vote of confidence is overwhelming."

Overhead there was the blare of a proximity alert, and the light on the bulkheads near the rear of the plane changed from red to green.

"Bashir!" Stewart called. "Get down here."

Unfastening my harness, I took lurching steps toward the security team where they were doing last-minute checks on their gear and parachutes.

My stomach clenched as the reality of my situation sunk in. *I'm about to jump out of a perfectly functioning airplane to save the world.*

I'd be tandem jumping with Hadlynne since I had no experience with skydiving and wanted to be more than a stain on the desert floor. The soldier seemed as excited about the whole business as I was, his complexion the same color as fresh milk.

"Any advice?" I asked as we strapped ourselves together, my back to his chest. I had to crane my neck to see his face in my periphery.

Hadlynne looked at me. "Don't chuck your breakfast."

I hadn't even thought about vomiting. I was more focused on not going splat, but now that he mentioned it, I felt a twinge of nausea.

"What happens if I do?"

"You lose your breakfast I get an early lunch." He tugged down on a strap harder than it probably needed.

"Thanks for that." I wrinkled my nose in disgust and focused straight ahead. Trust a soldier to provide a crude comment in any situation.

"Everyone tight?" Stewart bellowed. He ran a critical eye over the assembled team.

"As your mother, Sarge!" the team shouted in unison.

My jaw dropped at their coordinated insult. I half expected Stewart to throw a punch at someone, but his weathered features broke into a genuine smile. He looked over the team one last time and then nodded approvingly.

"Let's go kill a god then!"

The bay doors opened as another siren blared. Ahead was nothing but a howling sky and a blurry seam of darkness--the land below. My heart hammered, my knees turned watery and my stomach lurched. I might have felt embarrassed at my sudden rush of weakness but I was too busy trying not to be sick.

The others, like rugby players rushing for the tackle, surged out in a mob.

I wasn't so keen, but with Hadlynne grunting at my back, I had little choice.

For a moment I really wished I was going with Sark and Daria to land at the airport north of the compound. I opened my mouth to scream, but it was too late as the wailing sky opened up to swallow me.

The descent to the valley floor was a strange combination of terror and serenity.

I plummeted through the air, every instinct ramrodding terrified adrenaline through my veins. My arms splayed out, hands grasping at emptiness as the wind scoured my skin. Seconds ticked by, the ground growing closer but only so much that I knew I was moving, even if it seemed slowly. As time passed, the rushing in my blood faded enough that I realised I wasn't going to die just yet, and my pulse stabilized.

The security team kept close to each other as they descended, and I saw--to my horror--more than one of the loons grinning ear to ear. As seconds and metre after plummeting metre clipped by, I realised there was a certain thrilling peace to the whole thing.

Death may or may not come, and even if it did, there seemed little I could do to stop it. In the meantime, I let the elation of soaring through the air finally come in. It was something foundational, perhaps going back to when my father tossed me up into the air as a tot. It was never the rise that thrilled me, but surrendering to the plummet, certain I would land safe in my father's arms. The reflection of my father struck me squarely, as all thoughts of my parents did, but here at what might be my last moments, it somehow felt right.

The moment of our descent stretched on pleasantly, and then Stewart barked something, and I felt Hadlynne dragging us away from the others and into position.

"Brace yourself," he growled in my ear over the whistling wind.

It was then I learned two things.

The opening of a parachute is not the gentle blooming of fabric I'd imagined, and even with it open overhead, you still descend with unseemly speed.

Hadlynne and I jerked back as the chute opened, the force of deceleration enough to pop my neck and clack my teeth together. My senses were filled with cottony static for an instant from the jolt, and then I came to, realising how much closer the ground was.

We did slow, moving in a winding path downward, but as each revolution passed and the earth below grew uncomfortably nearer, fresh fear rose inside me. We had to slow down more than this, didn't we? The wind whistling against my skin had to be a sign that we were about to smash into the ground, which looked more like bedrock than a feather bed.

"Shouldn't we slow down?" I shouted.

"We're on target," Hadlynne offered mildly.

I wanted to scream that I didn't want to be on target, I wanted to land safely. I was a person, not a missile.

The ground jumped up to meet us, and then we were scudding across it. For a second I wondered if this was what roadkill felt like, before we came to an unceremonious stop.

After we disentangled, I emerged from the web of parachute and harness to behold the primeval lands that had birthed Ninurta.

The winds whipped across the landscape, which, despite all my previous assumptions about the region, was wet, cold, and sported darkly glistening vegetation. In the briefings Stewart mentioned the foothills being sodden with winter rains but I had still been expecting something more desert-like.

The rest of the team had smooth landings and in a few seconds we were assembled into a marching order by Stewart.

"All intel indicated that they dinna patrol or have picket lines beyond sentries at the compound." Stewart paced around as he spoke low but clear, gaze probing the terrain. "But we all know the truth about intel."

A few grunted in agreement while others nodded grimly.

"What's that about intel?" I whispered to Hadlynne.

"N'telligence is al'ys wrong, and when it ain't it's too late to matter."

"Minimal casualties," Stewart spat. "Both with contacts and your sorry selves. Secure any contact, whether they're eight or eighty. Watch yourselves and keep clear of the Angel when she gets to work."

More nods and a few raised chins my way from the team.

Angel? I felt prouder to have been given that name by these rough men than by any other accolade I'd earned. My shoulders squared a little.

I thought of Jackie and Marcus, how to explain how I was feeling; thinking about what they must be going through. I shook the thoughts away, knowing that distraction at this point could be the last mistake I made. Stewart was finishing his instruction, and I was missing it.

"... don't want dead heroes, I want live soldiers, lads. If anyone has a chance to stop this business, it's us here and now!"

He met every gaze with his frosty blue eyes before cracking one of his rare smiles.

"Right, move out and let's crack this noot!"

---

"WHAT THE..." came an awed, anonymous whisper as we crested the last hill. "Look at the size of it."

An enormous ziggurat sprawled across the valley floor, its corners touching the arms of the mountain that cradled it. It was made from dark grey stone, shiny and nearly black with the recent rains; a squat idol of a primordial demon-god, the tiered steps rising up as ridges of a scaly body, the shrine at its zenith a brutish crown. With every step we took down the slope, it seemed to grow: a construction that belonged to another time, though we knew it had been built in the last few days.

"Keep it tight," Stewart growled through the radio as he ranged at the front of the formation just behind the point squad.

The land was rougher here and every boulder seemed to promise an ambush. We crept along, unopposed, skirting the bare valley floor. The wind continued to howl, hampering our hearing somewhat, but we heard no alarm.

Did Ninurta really have such confidence that he didn't bother to set a watch?

The moaning whistle of the wind faded as we approached the wide stairs on the western face of the ziggurat. In its absence a steady rhythm rose, backed by the trilling of pipes and the strum of stringed instruments. Intermingled was a low chant, almost a whisper.

My arms prickled with goose bumps, and a chill rolled down my spine like ice water.

The point squad reported all-clear for the short sprint across the valley floor to the stairs. From there, it was only a matter of lugging ourselves up to the higher tiers where we anticipated Ninurta would be holding court.

We held, though, waiting for word from Daria and Sark that they had touched down and were nearing the approach from the other side.

"What do you think?" Stewart had shuffled back down the line to Hadlynne and me. "That madwoman o' yers goin' to come through?"

I shrugged. My body was tense from the undercurrent of power pressing against my mind. Gingerly I reached out my metallic awareness. Seams of copper answered back, so precisely ordered that they couldn't be natural, quivering in a latticework of metal within the stones of the ziggurat. The chant rose, and I felt I was going to be swept up in the undertow as the power drew inward and was funnelled down into the copper conduits, plunging down deep into the earth.

It was like a tide, surging with the rise and fall of the syllables of the chant, each time climbing a little higher. I leaned into it and felt hundreds of individual wills rushing past me to gather and plunge, all directed by an intelligence so focused it hurt to sense its raw intention. Ninurta was drawing power, the souls of his gathered offspring, and driving it like a spike into the earth.

"Somethin' bad is happening," Bordeaux observed, a ghost of fear an unnatural and unwelcome addition to his flinty voice. "We can't hang about."

"Steady on, man," Stewart warned gruffly, but then turned to lean close to my ear. "He's not wrong. We can all feel somethin' unnatural about, and we can't sit here with our thumbs up our arse."

I nodded, letting my metallic senses play across the network of copper, wondering if I could stymie the power being driven down. I was sure that so much power couldn't be stopped, but anything I could do to slow its descent or sap its strength would buy us time. We would have to risk alerting Ninurta.

"Keep an eye out." I held out my hand toward the ziggurat. "I'm going to make mischief."

The ground beneath our feet gave a tremble that turned my knees to jelly.

"Mischief accomplished, I ken," Stewart grunted.

"That wasn't me," I whispered, unable to keep the fear out of my voice. "I think it's already started."

Stewart's face paled and clenched until veins throbbed at his temples.

"Then we're goin' in," he growled, turning toward the ziggurat with a look of sheer loathing.

"Wait," I called as he stomped off, orders rumbling in his chest to match the last echoes of the shuddering earth. "I think I can disrupt the metal conducting the power downward."

Stewart didn't stop moving, calling over his shoulder. "Good, do that while we advance."

Sweat sprang up on my brow as I reached out to the veins of copper in the ziggurat, probing for weak points.

"You don't understand! I'm not sure if it will destabilise the structure. It doesn't do anyone any good if you're crushed by a collapsing pyramid."

Stewart seemed about to argue but paused at a sharp breath from me when I felt a souring influence that could only be Kezsarak sliding along one of the further branches of the ziggurat. The copper began to twist and rupture as the corruptive infection spread along the widening web of metal. On the next wave of tidal power the conduit was not up to the task: a series of tiny ruptures, cascaded outward in a dazzling and terrifying display.

Before I could share what I was sensing, there was a tremendous crack as though the earth was shattering pottery, and the entire ziggurat shivered. Some stones fell away, mammoth blocks as big as four-door sedans tumbled like children's blocks to the valley floor. Other stones splintered and shifted leaving jagged lines spider webbing across the structure as the last of Ninurta's harnessed power grounded out through the structure. Dust and rubble billowed between open seams in the stone. I ducked my head against the storm of debris as it spread over the valley floor, pelting us with bits of stone and grains of metal.

The structure settled into its new state, stones giving low, protesting groans as the last bits of rubble skittered and skipped down to the ground. Then there was only silence, an oppressive quiet, even the wind holding its breath.

"That's your cue, my dear," Daria's voice came over the radio in defiance of the stillness.

"You heard her lads!" Stewart roared. "Move it!"

Without time to consider, I ran across the plain with the team.

And just like that, the battle to save the world had begun.

# NINETEEN

Stairs had to be the greatest way to end heroics before they'd ever begun.

By the time we reached the top tier, after twenty minutes of laborious and treacherous climbing, even the fittest of the team was red-faced and gulping down air. I was an utter wreck, my legs trembling, my back throbbing, as I wheezed with each step. Steadying hands on my back from teammates had kept me whole and moving upward.

Not exactly how I wanted to go into the fight of my life, but the team was already ranging ahead of me through the maze-like assemblage of pillars and altars. Many of them held fistfuls of zip-ties and tasers; the combat rifles slung over their backs as a last resort.

"Cover!" Hadlynne snapped, dragging me behind a pillar.

A mob of armed men and women came jogging toward us from one of the many passages that led deeper into the ziggurat. I felt a thrill of fear, knowing that if they spotted us or headed after the team, this could all be over.

Pushing aside my fatigue and steadying my breathing to rhythmic gasps. I stretched out my metallic senses, attaching a mental hook to weapons. It took me longer than I wanted, there were so many of them. Fortunately, the Winterthür agents didn't seem to be in any hurry.

"What're they waitin' for?" Hadlynne hissed. His combat rifle already in hand.

Latching onto the last gun in the mob, I braced myself against the pillar, settling my mind. But as I gathered energy for the heavy pull I realised the weapons hadn't moved an inch; all were hanging loosely on straps or in hands.

*That doesn't make sense.*

Shouts and screams – orders and fear – echoed from the interior. I needed to get in there.

I turned to Hadlynne and put a finger to my lips before sliding quietly to steal a quick glance around the pillar.

The entire mob just stood there, arms hanging at their sides, staring at nothing in particular with eyes as black as pitch.

With a start, I remembered the packs of snarling men Daria had sent after us at Museum Station. It was clear the Winterthür agents had succumbed to the same demonic trick.

"It's alright." I stepped out from cover despite Hadlynne's bewildered expression.

As one, the mob turned and looked at me. The sudden attention of their black eyes left my mouth dry, and my heart in my throat, but I forced myself to straighten and look at them directly, channelling a little of Stewart's commanding presence.

"Daria sent you?" I asked.

With uncanny coordination, they nodded in unison.

"Did she give you instructions?"

Dozens stared on, unblinking and unmoving.

"Uh ... did she tell you to follow my orders?"

The heads bobbed together with insectile precision.

"What the bloody hell?" Hadlynne muttered. He stepped from behind the pillar.

More cries reminded me that there was a battle going on.

"Right, you lot are going to transport prisoners and the wounded off this little hill."

Again the unsettling synchronised nod.

"Help the security team as they come." As an afterthought I added, "You won't be needing these to do that."

I yanked the weapons from their limp grasps, staggering a few as the straps tugged free of their slack shoulders. A tangled ball of firearms drifted towards me as I turned back to the thoroughly befuddled Hadlynne.

"Daria's put them under some sort of spell." I jerked my head toward the assembled thralls. "At least they are out of the way."

"Could they fight?"

"Probably. But I don't know how long Daria's hold lasts or how strong it is. I'd rather have them unarmed and out of the way than armed and possibly turning in the middle of the fight."

"Fair 'nuff," He nodded then cast an eye to the floating pile of guns. "Best pick yer cream o' that lot, then let's move. Still got to addle our brass in this fight."

I shook my head at the Yorkshireman, a smile spreading across my face.

"I'm getting the cream right now."

Streams of liquid metal flowed toward me, crawling up my body to form armour and wings.

---

HADLYNNE and I worked our way inwards, passing several of the security team securing knots of Inconquo-blooded. They looked around as though struggling to shake off a dream. Their hands were bound and they were frog-marched toward the ziggurat stairs. I searched for Uncle Iry among their number, but a scream of men in pain forced me to rush on ahead.

Two of the security team were frantically prying at the barrels of their combat rifles, now wrapped around their throats. Their faces were beginning to purple as a slight teenager wearing only a pair of athletic shorts stood over them, a cruel grin spread over his deeply tanned face.

I sent two blades of thought to part the barrels and gather the metal to me as Hadlynne fired his taser. The paired darts were millimetres from the youth's skin when the Inconquo snared them in midair.

That was impressive, as even I struggled with fast-moving projectiles. The teen's glee turned to rage at our interruption of his fun. My metal-shod body shot forward as two of my wings arced overhead like twin scorpion tails.

The young Inconquo's eyes widened, and he threw himself backward, at the same time his power lashed out to drive the wings away. He may have been quick, but even without the rings, I had more raw power. With the rings, he could no more stop me than if he kicked a football to stop a speeding car. The wings thumped into his chest, knocking him flat.

I landed with a clang of bronze encased heels hitting stone. As I wrapped steel wreathed fingers around his throat something ugly and hateful twisted behind his eyes, and I felt a will behind his push against me.

The youth squirmed in my metal-hardened grip as I looked into his eyes and felt Ninurta, or at least part of him, staring back at me.

"I'm coming for you, old man," I snarled.

I felt Ninurta's will rush into this unfortunate vessel, but my armoured head snapped forward into the Inconquo's face, and the lad fell from my hand poleaxed.

Hadlynne secured the unconscious boy's bonds while the two security team members got to their feet massaging their throats. They motioned us onward. I spared a glance at the young bloodied face, but I didn't have time to wonder how much had been Ninurta and how much had been the boy.

Hadlynne let me take lead as we continued toward the centre of the ziggurat. Ten-foot tall statues of gods and monsters, worked from various metals, were like shrines ringing the broad stone walkway that encircled a bowl-shaped depression.

Screams continued to echo around us and I felt the ripples and psychic pressures of wills at work. I tried to pinpoint them and gauge their strength, but there was too much movement by foreign minds. Then my metallic sense drew my attention to something else: a will that had to be Ninurta's. A level of power and control I could never dream of was knitting the exploded seams of copper together again. The thorough devastation of Kezserak's fury made the work slow, but soon it would be repaired enough for Ninurta to resume channelling power toward the Earth's core.

Time was slipping through our fingers.

A group of Inconquo-blooded staggered up from the centre of the ziggurat, looking as confused as those we'd seen earlier.

A massive blow smashed me to the ground, knocking the breath from my body. My metal-encased frame was driven down hard enough to crack stone; only instinctive reinforcements and the power of the rings kept me from becoming paste.

A stout woman in workman's coveralls appeared, holding a crudely fashioned club of bronze sized right for an ogre. Her power thrummed through the metal weapon raised for a blow meant to drive me into the basement of the ziggurat.

There was a sharp snap and the two wired barbs of a taser landed in her side. The club fell from her grip, landing heavily enough that I felt the impact through the stones. A second later the woman herself folded over, her body curling up like paper before a flame.

"Thanks," I said as my wings propelled me to my feet.

Hadlynne nodded in recognition, beginning to smile, but the expression died on his face as his eyes bulged at the sight of something behind me.

I whirled, wings raised. An enormous grey foot stomped down on me. My wings interlocked to form a hedge of protection, even as the towering body behind the foot bore down. Sparks flew off my metal appendages as they were ground down, forcing me into a crouch.

The pressure redoubled, but I drove two of my wings down into the stone and the braced shield held. Metallic senses reported that I was under attack by one of the immense statues, composed mostly of tin and being driven by an Inconquo who'd hollowed out a space inside.

The percussive chatter of a rifle firing reached my ears over the screech of metal on metal.

"Oi, eyes up ye ketty bast'rd!" Hadlynne roared before another blast from his weapon. "T'ink yer 'ard do yeh? I'm Sammy Hadlynne, 'ardest baller ever was! Learn me name! Sammy! Hadlynne!"

The rifle barked again, shots *plinking* off of the statue.

He had to know he couldn't hurt the statue, but as the pressure slackened I understood. More shots rebounded off the statue, and the huge mass of metal turned toward Hadlynne, cocking the foot to one side.

All six wings flared outward as I seized the opportunity and propelled myself out from under the foot. Taking to the air, I swept around to smash feet-first into the statue's chest. The metal figure gave a groan and I rode it down to the stones as it toppled backward. A spiderweb of cracks bloomed out from under the fallen colossus.

Channelling burning streams of willpower into two wings, I excited the molecules until they glowed with forge-heat. They swept downward, carving through the tin arms rising to bat me away, leaving smoking stumps. I felt the Inconquo within the statue losing focus and seized upon the weakness, plunging both wings into the dented chest. Molten tin bubbled and spat as I ripped the statue's chest open. As my prying wings reached the cavity where the Inconquo hid, I felt their hold on the metal sever like a cord being snapped. With a final roar of exertion, I split the statue open and watched a small grey-haired woman in a stained business suit tumble out. Her body was limp, but her narrow chest rose and fell gently as she lay on the splintered stonework.

Hadlynne's cheer was cut short by an awful crunching sound.

Spinning, I saw the stout woman tottering, hands wrapped around the cudgel that was atop Hadlynne's broken body.

A defiant, vengeful scream tore from my throat and my power reached out to yank the bludgeon from the woman. I didn't care if her hands came with it, so hot was my wrath.

But the club didn't fly into my hands like it should have.

It lurched up into the air then hung there, still in her hands but suspended between her power and mine. Grinding my teeth I pulled harder, and the club bearer staggered a few steps toward me, but then a fresh push of will stopped her advance. Blood began to seep from her eyes and nose from the strain, and past her crimson tears I again saw Ninurta, sneering at me.

"Monster," I spat and slammed my will down with all the force the rings could muster.

The club twisted and then came apart with the screech of shearing metal. The Inconquo crumpled, blood flowing freely as her eyes rolled up into her skull.

I raced over to Hadlynne, but before I knelt at his side I could see that he was gone. He stared vacantly toward the centre of the ziggurat. I forced myself to follow his gaze. My heart ached, and my soul was sick, but I had a job to do. I whispered my thanks as I rose and swore that his death would mean something.

My wings opened and I took to the air to sail down into the ziggurat's heart, an angel descending into the devil's domain.

# TWENTY

Ninurta sat on his throne frantically fusing seams of copper together.

The depression formed a kind of amphitheatre around him. Knots of Inconquo-blooded milled about, still under Ninurta's stupefying compulsion. They looked up at me with faces torn between bewilderment and terror. When Ninurta and I came to blows, his spell would not hold and they would flee.

I could not afford distraction, so I fought the urge to look for Uncle Iry.

Now I had to trust that Daria and Sark were near enough for this to work. I kept two wings folded protectively in front while the other four beat the air with thrumming strokes.

"Ninurta!"

The demigod looked up, resplendent in his ancient finery of robes and decadent jewellery. His cruel mouth twisted into a hungry smile as he reclined in his throne and leered up at me.

"Pretty birds belong in pretty cages." He cocked one arm up on the arm of his throne and rested his head upon gilded knuckles. "I wondered where you'd flown off to, little one, but I am glad to see that you've come back to me."

I settled in the air a handful of metres above him, glaring down at his attempt at nonchalance. I could feel his mind withdrawing the foundations. He could croon and chuckle all he wanted, but he knew he was in for a fight.

"This ends now," I declared, raising my voice to fill the amphitheatre. "The madness, the death, the domination. All of it stops today."

Ninurta threw back his head and laughed. "Really? You act as though I am an evil tyrant to be toppled, but your modern world is infested with a thousand petty despots. Small men and women with small ambitions. I am not here to oppress humanity, but to save it. If you could humble yourself and open your eyes, you would see the truth."

Now it was my turn to laugh. "A megalomaniac talking about humility. Now there's an informed opinion."

Ninurta shook his head and slowly rose from his throne, linen robes flowing around his powerful frame like an ivory waterfall. "I am not a proud man, just an honest one."

He gestured at the huddling groups around the amphitheatre. "Humanity has lost its way. It fell from the path of ascension that began with me. One of evolution's million failures. For all its marvels and toys, humanity is merely a collection of apes beating their chests at what they can bully and cowering from what they cannot."

He looked up, his face pleading. His voice was soft, rich and pained, as if his heart was breaking. "I deserve better, you deserve better, and indeed all of humanity deserves better. So I will set things right, even if I must bear the burden, the crushing weight that such choices require. If there is to be any hope for our species, someone must dare to reach for a brighter future no matter the consequences."

This was a monster's justification, the sort of lie a fanatic told himself to escape responsibility for his actions. I wanted to rebut, but I didn't want to give him the satisfaction of knowing I'd even listened his ramblings.

"You talk too much." I crossed my arms over my chest. "Why don't you get to dropping meteors already."

Ninurta shook his head at the taunt, sparing me a condescending smile. "I don't think anything as dramatic as that is called for," he replied. "And you should listen with more than just your ears, Inconquo."

There was an eruption of broken stone, and four kraken worthy tentacles of copper burst from the floor around his throne to reach for me.

I hadn't sensed him drawing some of the seams up from the ziggurat's bowels, but the fact that he was desperate enough to use them to attack me, despite their importance to his plan, put a smile on my face as I dodged the flailing metal.

I darted around one, slipped by a second, and managed to deflect a third with my wings before the fourth tendril sent me spinning toward the floor. I tried to right myself, but the other tendrils rallied to buffet me over and over until I crashed down before the throne.

Ninurta sprang down the last few steps, landing in front of me, light and agile as a cat, and then kicked me squarely in my armoured face. Even protected, my head snapped back with the force of the blow, and I went tumbling over my wings. I skidded to a stop, my wings biting into the stone floor and forcing me upright.

"You'll have to do better than that." I straightened my wings with a flex of mental power and faced him squarely.

The four tendrils slithered back into their holes.

"Oh. I think you know I can."

A flash of metallic awareness saved me and I sprang into the air a fraction of a second before the tendrils erupted again, opening a yawning hole in the floor where I had been standing. I accelerated upward as they flailed after me before turning sharply and diving down into their midst.

I heated two of my wings with that searing power again, thankful that the tempered steel from the firearms could withstand the incredible temperatures. I hacked and hewed as I spun and bounced amongst the writhing tendrils. The copper did not succumb like the tin, but with each stroke it warped and began to run. I shunted a thrust of mental power through the rings to drive the tendrils into one another; within seconds they became a knotted clinging mass, twisting violently against itself.

A hiss of frustration rose from Ninurta as he reached out to disentangle the tendrils. Knowing I had scant seconds, I burst out from the morass and made a beeline for the distracted demigod.

Two blazing wings in front, two ready to shield me, and two churning the air, I piled into him with all I could muster. The blazing wings cut smouldering gashes in his robes before lodging in his shoulders, pinning his arms back, as my armoured fists drove into his chest. I savoured his look of surprise as I drove him back toward his throne. His foot struck against the steps and he fell, landing hard on his back with a clang.

Digging the sharp tips of my wings deeper in to his metal-infused flesh, I prepared to pile-drive a fist into his face.

With a wet, bestial snarling sound he twisted underneath me, wrenching free at the same time kicking upward. Committed to my heavy swing, the kick between my legs sent me crashing into the steps fist first as he slid out from under me. The impact would have snapped bones had it not been for my protective shell, but pain radiated up my arm and into my shoulder, making me grit my teeth.

Before I could rise, Ninurta sprang on my exposed back, gathering my wings like flower stems in huge hands. I tried to twist away, to swivel my wings, to break free or at least stab at him but his grip, both physical and mental, was inescapable. Metal squealed and tines snapped with sharp *plinks* as his grip tightened. I kicked while scrambling for purchase on the stone, but he laughed at my feeble efforts before raising me up by my wings to smash me against the steps.

The first impact struck like a gong. My armour held. But he slammed me down again, and again, until I felt like battered jelly inside my dented armour and the stone of the steps caked me in a fine powder.

"I don't think you will need these anymore," he growled next to my ear in that awful leonine voice. I tried to form thoughts to fight back, but all I could do was keep the metal around me by sheer instinct. He planted a foot on my back, bearing down as he pulled upward.

I held onto the twisted metal that had been my wings as hard as I could, but felt my hold coming apart millimetre by millimetre. I heard metal tearing a second before my will gave way. My mind staggered, reeling as an aching numbness washed over me and I blacked out.

I came to as I crashed down next to the wound in the floor where the mangled copper tendrils still writhed. Skidding across the stones, my metal skin kicked up sparks.

"You could have been a queen!"

I looked up with bleary eyes to see Ninurta stalking forward, muscles rolling with predatory elegance. "I offered you the world, and you rejected it."

Despite the rings channelling inward, I was recovering more quickly than I had any right to. Control over my armour was awkward, the metal shell stiffened in places, making my motions jerky.

He loomed over me, a colossus of muscle and bone, every fibre having the strength of steel. Swelling behind his incredible physical presence was the shadow of his titanic power. I was hopelessly, absurdly, outmatched.

"Ungrateful insect." His voice was as flat and cold as a razor blade.

He reached out, pushing past my defence, rings or not. His fingers sank into the gunmetal skin as though it were cloth, twisting the brass frame beneath so it bit into my skin. I lashed out with sharp kicks that rang off his shins and knees with dull clangs.

He drilled down into the fabric of the armour and severed my connection with a single savage twist of power. I looked into his chilling stare and saw nothing but contempt as he tore the metal skin from my body in one sharp pull. The metal parted like rotten lace, small spurs raking my arms and face.

I reeled backward and realised with horror that I was at the edge of the tunnel where the tendrils writhed. My heels scuffed the jagged edge.

Before I could right myself, Ninurta's hand shot out and closed around my throat. He drew me from the edge and off my feet to look him in the eye. My fingers dug at his crushing fingers as my legs kicked feebly, but I might as well have been clawing at an iron vice.

"You are unworthy. Unworthy of my time, my attention, and my blood." Ninurta bent his head forward to place his lips next to my ears.

"Die knowing you were not enough," Ninurta whispered as his fingers began to tighten. "Die knowing you failed."

# TWENTY-ONE

The pressure on my neck, the tissue of my throat, the bones of my spine, was so incredible I had a fleeting thought that I was about to explode. Then the pressure was gone and I was falling.

*Is this what it's like to die?*

I landed on the stone floor hard enough to make my teeth rattle and raw, hacking gasps rocked me. I forced myself to my hands and knees to give my greedy lungs as much room as they needed to claim the oxygen they had been denied. I looked up at Ninurta with tear-bleared eyes.

Every sinew stood out as his body like an electric current was passing through him; his teeth bared in a frothing grimace. Across his taut neck, a bloom of black veins stood out like venomous vines burrowing into the trunk of a tree. From those tumorous growths a shadow tentacle of an edimmu stretched behind the stricken demigod to Daria standing a few paces away. Ninurta had been so intent on me he didn't notice when a living darkness separated itself from the shadows of the throne, rearing back like a black serpent ready to strike.

"I've been waiting for this day for a long, long time," Daria hissed through jagged fangs.

A hard hand seized my arms and hauled me to my feet. I looked up and saw Sark's demon-ravaged face, but he wasn't even looking at me. His eyes were fixed on Ninurta, and I could hear the grinding engine pulse inside his chest building momentum. Kezsarak's voice bubbled up from deep within, a poisonous, hateful noise that stung my ears.

*TRAITOR*

Still fighting for air, I remembered the ancient history between Kezsarak and Ninurta. Ninurta had convinced Kezsarak to aid him against the demon's father Asag, but despite his promises to the contrary, Ninurta had slain Asag and set the *gallu* on the path to madness and damnation. Kezsarak's hatred of humanity in general, and the Inconquo, in particular, all began with Ninurta.

"Remember the plan, Sark," I croaked. "We're so close. Remember."

Sark's gaze didn't leave the demigod, but his cracked lips quivered, and he ran a pale tongue over them.

"Hurry, Ibby," he whispered hoarsely. "I'm not sure how long we can hold him."

We? Oh no! If Sark and Lowe were working together and could barely keep the demon at bay, things could come undone just before the finish line.

Pulling from his nerveless grip, I staggered a few steps away from the demigod and the gaping black pit. The copper had sunk back down into the depths without Ninurta's will to animate it.

"Not yet, Kezsarak," I gasped, as I fought to slow my pounding heart and steady my laboured breathing. I had one shot at this.

"Hurry!"

Lowe's voice revived me, and with hardening focus I drove my metallic awareness into Ninurta's rigid body. I plunged deep and found the nebula of living metal, its movement sluggish, slowed by Daria's poison. It was a testament to his terrible will that it still flowed at all. It quickened and pulled against me: even against the crippling demonic poison of an edimmu the demigod fought on.

The rings before me, I poured everything I had into drawing the living metal out of him. At first it felt like trying to drag a mountain, but with agonising slowness, the current began to bow and turn my way. A fresh coat of sweat broke out across my body and stung my eyes as I dug deep, pulling from depths I didn't know I had.

Crimson motes sprang from the demigod's skin and a tight, impotent scream of rage slipped from between Ninurta's teeth. Sark stalked forward, Kezsarak's demonic heartbeat hammering like an engine ready to explode.

*TRAITOR!*

"Not yet!" Daria shouted, muscles standing out on her neck. "She has to draw it all out. Not yet!"

The stream of bloody particles coming off Ninurta grew by the second, coalescing into a flickering cloud. I could already sense places in Ninurta where the choruses of metal had gone silent.

"Almost ... there!" I snarled through clenched teeth. "Almost!"

Sark lurched forward, hand outstretched, his body recoiling as though he was trying to pull away from a fire.

"Sark, no!" I screamed. "Almost—"

*VENGEANCE!*

Sark's hand plunged into the swirling motes, fingers curling into a gnarled claw. The sour tang of Kezsarak's corrupting influence spread like wildfire, and the red turned to black. The glimmers of metal turned to bleak stars flashing with lethal promise. I knew what was coming as my grip came undone and the last particles of living metal were drawn back into Ninurta.

The catastrophic detonation came, and time seemed to slow to a crawl even as the sparks bloomed into fireballs. Sark's eyes bulged in terror as a mad, rambling laugh burst from his lips. Daria's grip on Ninurta withered before the surge of heat and light. I reared back, certain I was dead.

A silver silhouette detached itself from Sark with a sound like ripping parchment. The figure stretched into the shape of a tall and lanky man. Pearly translucent arms enveloped me. The shade's touch was cold yet comforting, an embrace that soothed and steadied me.

*I will hold you.*

The voice was the rich, articulate tones of a century-old ghost and a very dear friend.

The fireballs swelled, as time returned to normal, devouring everything they touched. Heat and force wash over me, but I felt little more than a summer breeze. I squeezed my eyes shut as the explosion grew bright as the sun.

*I won't let you go.*

Flashes of heat prickled across my skin, slipping through as the force of the blast tore at the protective layer Lowe had created around me, but the breaches mended even as I felt Lowe's grip slacken.

The seconds stretched and Lowe's grip thinned into a bare caress as more and more of him was ripped away by the fury he was holding at bay. The final aftershock of the eruption rolled by and dragged away the last traces of Lowe's spirit.

*I'm so proud of you.*

Then he was gone.

---

BLINKING in the wake of Kezsarak's fatal error, I stood on unsteady legs and looked around.

An ache like a piece of my heart was missing throbbed in my chest and I wanted to crumple to the ground and weep. My gaze swung left and right, seeing things without understanding, hearing things without comprehending.

Lowe was gone and Ninurta survived. How could this happen, the plan had been ...

Ninurta survived!

The world snapped into focus and I heard a scream of pain accompanied by the hiss of searing heat.

I spun around and saw Ninurta, ravaged and burned to a nightmare, sinking his fingers into the exposed metal throbbing in Sark's chest. Sark shrieked as the grinding gears of Kezsarak's infernal engine whined and snarled. More of Ninurta's flesh peeled away as he sank his hand up to the wrist, revealing bones that glimmered with a metal sheen.

"So close, Kezsarak," Ninurta rasped, his voice a ragged sound in his scorched throat. "So very close."

The demigod's hand closed around something inside Sark's chest and his scream rose then crashed into a breathless groan. Ninurta's hand gave a sharp twist and withdrew. Sark collapsed to the floor and stared upward, his mouth working soundlessly. He shuddered and went limp, a puppet with its strings cut.

In Ninurta's hand, dripping molten metal was a heart. Around the metallic organ, a shuddering shadow, almost like a lightless flame flickered and shrank. The sound of Kezsarak's hellish motor coughed a final turn and then fell silent as the shadowy flame extinguished.

Ninurta gargled a laugh and tossed the heart over his shoulder into the pit.

Daria, her human guise in tatters, crouched next to me. Just like Pierre, the creature beneath the beautiful woman's skin was a black-skinned horror; but also like him, the power of

Lamashtu's curse knit her back together. When most of her human face had reappeared, I was surprised to see neither fear nor sadness. In that instant, looking into her eyes, I saw acceptance, even peace.

"Why can't any of you fools understand?" Ninurta drew my attention back to his skeletal hulk, all that remained of the once magnificent king. "I am unstoppable. I am irresistible. I am perpetual!

He threw a hand toward his feet and with an enraged bellow launched his will outward and downward simultaneously. I felt it like a rip-tide and was nearly drawn into the undertow. Bracing myself against it, I realised others were not so lucky. The wills, the very life energy, of the other Inconquo-blooded were being dragged from beyond the temple walls to fuel his downward questing blast. It was not as clean or elegant as the ritual, and I felt wills snapping like the Inconquo with the bronze club, their minds and bodies buckling under the strain.

Ninurta would have his new world, even if he had to kill all of his descendants to do it.

I reached out, trying to divert his efforts, but it was like trying to redirect a flooding river. I was more likely to get dragged in than I was to change its course, much less stop it.

I turned to Daria, despair welling up, and saw a sad smile spreading across her face. She reached out and clasped my hands in hers.

As the earth beneath us began to shake, she said, "I'm glad it will end this way, and I'm glad it will be with you."

I wanted to argue, to tell her not to give up, but I was beaten, nearly broken, and so tired. I stared at her as she bent her head and kissed my hands. Something small, cylindrical, and feeling of earth slid into my hand before she pulled away.

Daria turned back towards Ninurta, her eyes gleaming fiercely.

"You look ragged and weary, o' king of kings." Tendrils of darkness spread around her. "Come rest in my embrace!"

Ninurta looked up and a rictus grin spread across his face. He moved to meet the edimmu, even as his will continued to drag in more Inconquo essence to power his assault upon the earth's core. Another shudder shook the ziggurat.

Ninurta laughed as he batted the clutching cords of night away, but Daria was not satisfied to lash at him from a distance. Shrieking like a hellcat, she threw herself on him, fingers curling into claws as her mouth sprouted a nest of fangs. He punched forward, hitting her squarely in the chest. Despite this, her black claw fingers dug at his flesh, finding enough purchase to climb up his arm. Loosing a shrill war-cry, her human disguise sloughed off like an old garment as she scrambled up his body. The demigod roared like an enraged beast, gripping at her but only ever managing to pull great fistfuls of ichor away.

"Now, Ibby!" Daria cried before snapping her head forward and driving hooked fangs into Ninurta's flesh. Many broke off with grinding cracks, but a handful pierced skin and notched into bones.

With a drunken start, I remembered she had placed something in my hand. I recognised the small clay cylinder, its entire length engraved in a spidery web of cuneiform: Daria's phylactery.

Ninurta gripped Daria by the back of her head, wrenching her back. Teeth snapped, tumbling free or remaining lodged in his chest. In answer, she lashed out with tentacles of living darkness, dragging herself tight against his raw, exposed flesh. Her venom found no purchase in his alert and enraged psyche, but the physical darkness dug into him like meat hooks. So much metal had been taken that he couldn't protect all of himself, not anymore.

"Ibby, please!" Daria screamed, pulling until her mangled body was nearly within his wounds.

Grief, exhaustion, and pain had thickened my thoughts, but her urgent words punched through. I remembered Pierre Gwaffu's last terrible moments, the voice of Lamashtu, his terror, and then the fire. The fire.

My fingers closed around the construction of ancient clay, feeling it crumble even with a little pressure. Around me, I could feel the mounting power the demigod was driving deeper and harder. There was a trembling to the ground now, like a tuning fork ringing. Thousands of miles beneath my feet, the heart of the world trembled as it came under the grip of a monster. The time to act was almost gone.

Choking back a sob, I raised my ringed hand toward them, drawing the broken fragments of my armour and wings together. For an instant, as Ninurta's hand began to crush her skull, Daria twisted to look at me, one part of her face still human.

"Thank you," I gasped, and a smile formed on her face.

Then I crushed the phylactery.

The wild, hellish sounds of pig, donkey, lion, and dog crying out in unison rent the air. It seemed Lamashtu had been waiting. The announcing chorus filled the amphitheatre, spinning round and round, louder and louder until I dropped to my knees. I tried to cover both my ears, while I focused my will through the rings, launching the twisted metal scraps forward. Ninurta was a frenzy of twisting and struggling, but still Daria held on.

*"Oh my darling Daria, what have you brought me at last?"*

Even prepared for it, the Lamashtu's voice turned my stomach and left me shivering.

Ninurta roared a wordless cry of defiance until the metal struck him and Daria, pinning them together.

*"It took longer than I hoped, but immortality lets one be patient. Isn't that right, little king?"*

"You have no claim on me!" Ninurta screamed, real fear sharpening his booming voice. "I deny you, demon! I am the only god here!"

A laugh filled the amphitheatre, and the sound slithered up my spine and wrapped its barbed coils around my heart. The shadows streaming from Daria began to boil and Ninurta's movements grew jerky, his supreme grace overruled by panic. His will turned against me, trying to free himself from the crushing embrace of the metal that caged him and Daria together. On my knees, I threw everything I had into holding him and thwarting his power. Spots filled my vision and hot blood ran from my nose.

"Fools!" the demigod screamed as the first blossom of green flames sprang to life. "You stupid, ignorant fools! I am king of kings, I AM—"

"*MINE!*"

Lamashtu's exultant cry almost drowned out Ninurta and Daria's screams as the crackling jade flames enshrouding them. Ninurta's dying will thrust against me, not strong enough to free himself but strong enough to send him and Daria into the gaping hole in the floor. A blazing torch, their bodies indistinguishable amongst the flames...

# TWENTY-TWO

An awful grinding sound warned that the stone floor beneath me was starting to crack and shift. I forced myself into a lurching run. The cracks expanded across the floor and into the tiered steps above. As I mounted the first step a seam widened with shocking suddenness, creating a chasm wide enough to swallow me whole.

My body burned and throbbed with exhaustion. The long, crumbling path to the top filled me with despair. I'd never make it. Why die any more tired than I already was? Wasn't the battle won?

A shrill cry from above snapped me out of my morbid musing.

Two little girls had been thrown to a lower tier, which had now become an island. One look at their wide terrified eyes in their small terrified faces was all I needed.

"Get moving guardian!" I snarled as I pivoted and sprang back towards the pit that had swallowed Ninurta and Daria's burning remains.

Skidding to a stop at the very edge, I forced myself not to think about the shards of stone I'd sent spiralling down into the dark. My brain screamed at me to leave it alone; it was done. Strained beyond all reason I licked parched, bloodied lips and reached down into the dark.

Screaming with the effort, although the sound was hoarse and tremulous, I drove my ringed fist skyward as a tendril of copper rose from the pit. The copper bowed at my feet and I leaped on as I widened the head into a platform wide enough to accommodate several people.

Another shuddering rumble shook the ziggurat. Stones tumbled down. With more screams from the Inconquo-blooded, I knew my time was short.

I bid the copper rise, fighting the static at the back of my mind I knew meant unconsciousness, and therefore death. I might die from the exertion, but I was getting those people out of here.

The copper disc reached the crumbling tier where the girls huddled as it began to come apart.

"Jump!" I beckoned them with outstretched arms.

The girls stared as they clutched each other, too terrified to move. I moved toward the edge of the disc and felt my hold wobble as I fought to keep the disc level.

"Please, jump!" I moved the disc as close as I dared under that splitting piece of stone. If a chunk of falling stone hit the disc, it would be the end.

Sobbing, one of the girls took a step forward, dragging her sister.

A spur of stone fell away less than a metre from them and they screamed, recoiling again.

"Please!" I locked eyes with the one who had taken the first step. "You can do it!"

Dark eyes, huge and terrified, met my gaze, and I willed with all I could that whatever blood we shared would let me reach her, touch her.

*Jump. Jump and I won't let you fall.*

Her eyes still wide and teary, she nodded. With a whispered word to her sister they took one step, then another. More stone fell away and they cried out, but they inched toward the edge, almost there.

The ziggurat rumbled and the platform gave way as they leaped into the air.

---

I SETTLED into a sitting position to conserve energy as we glided over the collapsing ziggurat. For all the joy at saving the two girls, I was holding on by threads.

The last works of Ninurta sank into the hungry, vengeful earth. Massive stones slid, and towering idols tottered before falling into the yawning pit that stretched out from the centre of the structure. What had been built in days to last for millennia vanished in seconds. When the dust settled there would be nothing but rubble, and perhaps an echo of hubris.

I, an aspiring archaeologist, had a single thought as I bore witness to the fallout of Ninurta's grand scheme: good riddance. The world had enough monuments to tyrants and madmen. Let time and antiquity forget him.

We drifted clear of the billowing dust cloud and sailed out over the plain of the valley. I smiled to see the people gathered below, so many Inconquo-blooded spared, though not all had made it. There was a pang in my heart, but I felt a little hand squeeze my shoulder.

I looked up into the eyes of the brave one and a smile spread across her smooth features.

"You're right." I squeezed her fingers gently. "It could have been much worse."

Neither of the girls had spoken and I supposed there was a good chance neither spoke English, but somehow it didn't matter. Not now, anyway. They seemed to understand me just fine.

The congregation of Inconquo-blooded was being watched over by the TNC security team, well-armed shepherds looking over a human flock, but I couldn't see any of the Group of Winterthür agents.

I brought the copper disc down near a knot of the watchful soldiers ... and immediately blacked out.

Water, cold and insistently wet, brought me back around. Squinting into the dusky sky, I saw Stewart kneeling over me. His face bore the biggest smile I'd ever seen on any person, and it was such a rare sight on his dour face it took a second to convince myself I wasn't dreaming.

"The girls, the twins?"

"Safe, they're safe," Stewart said, his smile not budging an inch. "Turns out their pa was taken too and was all too happy to have 'em back. Just had to put a cherry on top, didn't you?"

"Something's wrong with your face, Sarge."

"You did it, lass!" He chuckled, and, in another unprecedented move, scooped me up into a fierce hug. "Can't believe it myself, and I dinna ken how, but you did it!"

Crushed against his barrel chest, I couldn't respond, but when he finally released me enough to let me breathe, I gave him a wry smile.

"You had no confidence in your guardian angel, eh?" I chuckled, fighting back a cough. Despite the shower of water, my mouth felt dry as bone, and my chest ached.

Stewart laughed and, with a casual display of strength, dragged me up to my unsteady feet. He kept one arm around me and with the other he handed me a canteen.

"Well..." The old Scot looked sheepish. "I always thought being a cynic was part of the job, I suppose."

"Until today?"

"Aye." He gave my shoulder a shake. "Until today. It's not every day some wee lass calls off armageddon, ya ken?"

"I ken." I took another large swig from the canteen.

"*Ibukun*!"

A voice, hoarse and desperate, called behind me, the name sticking in my heart. Only one living person in all the world said my name like that.

"*Ya binti!*" Uncle Iry cried as I whirled, searching for him. "*Ya habibti!*"

Jogging up the line of soldiers was Bordeaux, Uncle Iry cradled in his strong arms. Uncle Iry, thinner and more worn than ever, had his eyes fixed on me, one emaciated arm stretching towards me.

The canteen fell from my grip, and I tore away from Stewart so fast I nearly pulled him over. My legs were still unsteady, each step trembling up my body to make my teeth rattle. Twice I stumbled, fingers brushing the earth as I fought to stay upright.

"*A'am!*"

I reached Bordeaux as he slowed and lowered Uncle Iry to the ground.

"Oh, *a'am*," I sobbed as I wrapped my arms around him.

His arms slid around me, so frail and light, the grip of an old man.

"Ibby," he said, cheeks shining with tears. "I knew you would come. I knew you would save us."

My heart, despite the pain, loss, and the aftershocks of terror, felt only an aching relief. Victory had cost more than I'd ever imagined. In time it would all come crashing back and I'd have to process and heal. But for now: I was alive, the world was still spinning, and for the first time since their founding the Inconquo could live free of Ninurta's shadow.

That was something to smile about, no matter what lay ahead.

"It is over now?" Uncle Iry asked softly, his face tired and worry-lined. "We are safe?"

I looked down at him and smiled, wiping tears from his grizzled cheeks.

"Better than that, *a'am,*" I whispered, drawing him so close, I wasn't sure I would ever let him go. "We're free."

# EPILOGUE

Rapping my knuckles on Jody Marks' office door, she responded a moment later with her usual, "Come."

Opening the door, I almost ran into Stewart's back.

"I'll contact our asset in Tripoli and begin to make the arrangements," Stewart said before snapping off a salute and turning around.

Stepping aside before he marched over me, I smiled and nodded as he left. The crusty sergeant's expression didn't change as his eye fell on me, but he did tip me a wink.

"Ms Bashir."

"Sargeant." I touched my forehead as he passed and shut the door behind him.

Crossing to the chair in front of Marks' desk, I sat down and waited expectantly. She took off the glasses she was wearing, folded them and set them aside.

"How is the move going?" she asked. "Holloway Road, wasn't it?"

I nodded. I'd signed the lease for a new flat in Islington since my old place with Jackie wasn't going to be big enough for four. It was a little premature, since it was too soon after Jackie's surgery for her to come home, but I wanted to be all set up and ready by the time the private facility TNC had paid for gave her the okay to come home.

"Good." I crossed one leg over the other. "Marcus has healed enough to be able to handle some of the heavy lifting and Uncle Iry has been keeping us fed while we get organized."

"I hear that reports from Ms Davies' physical therapists are positive?"

My heart buoyed and I couldn't keep the smile from my face. "They won't make promises, but I can tell they have high hopes for her."

"Splendid." Marks tapped her fingers on the desk.

"You didn't call me in here in the middle of my holiday to discuss Jackie's health or ask about our new flat, so..." I gestured for her to get on with it.

She cleared her throat. "Quite right. You'll recall from an earlier conversation that TNC has a project we're setting up to execute in North Africa."

"I remember."

"Libya, to be precise. In the Acacus."

My brows arched with interest. "Land of the Tashwinat Mummy. Interesting."

Marks snapped her fingers, pointed at me and grinned. "That. That right there is why you're right for this job."

I cocked my head. "Sorry?"

"You've studied archaeology. You already know about sub-Saharan finds. How are your acting skills?"

"Uh..."

"You are perfect to convincingly play the part of an archaeologist, as a cover, while forwarding an agenda to facilitate the awakening of a supernatural we would then recruit."

I blinked at her, bemused.

She went on, ignoring my look of confusion. "You're a young woman, she's a young woman. You're an archaeologist, she's an aspiring archaeologist." Marks was speaking quickly, her eyes glittering with excitement. Whatever she was babbling about, she was all enthusiasm.

"Slow down. I never graduated, and who are we talking about?"

Marks tented her fingers on a file folder I hadn't yet noticed. "You must sign the agreement and accept the job before I can reveal the her identity." She then nodded at a front corner of her desk where a small tablet sat.

Annoyed, I leaned over and grabbed the device. Waking up the screen revealed a single document, a contract entitled *Project Tempest*. I skimmed it and looked back up at Marks before reading off a few lines.

"Project prep starts in two weeks, should be wrapped up before the end of summer, involves a trip to Canada, and the Tadrart Acacus via Tripoli and Alawenat."

My pulse quickened at the thought of visiting the Sahara. I'd laid the dreams of a career as an archaeologist aside after Inconquo abilities took over my life, but I still thought about it and missed it at times.

Marks shifted forward. "Imperative to the success of the plan is maintaining the appearance of a true archaeological dig..."

I looked up at Marks. "The *appearance* of an archaeology dig? Not a real one?"

"Everything will be as authentic as we can make it. We've even hired a genuine Field Director with excellent experience. There will only be one person on staff who is not aware that the dig is a front."

My jaw dropped. "All this effort to trick one person? Why?"

"It's for her own good, trust me. Well? Do you want in?" Her eyes gleamed with a kind of hunger. Her excitement was catching.

"Will it involve combat?"

Marks' smile faded. "Uh, not a lot, no. Perhaps a little faked danger with the local tribes. If it's more soldiering you're looking for, I might have something in Russia, but..."

I put up a hand. "No! No, you misunderstand. I don't want combat. I've had enough of it for now, thanks. Digging in the desert sounds like just the ticket."

She straightened. "So... you're in?"

At a glance, the project looked perfect. No combat, a visit to North Africa, an archaeological dig. I'd still have two weeks to get settled in our new flat, and I wouldn't be gone all that long, plus I didn't get paid if I didn't work, so..."

I nodded at Marks. "Hand me your stylus."

Her grin sparkled. "Great."

She waited while I signed the contract, then took the tablet and slipped it into a desk drawer.

Leaning forward, I took the folder as she slid it across the desk. Opening it revealed a dossier on a tanned young woman with dark hair and pale grey eyes. She looked barely out of her teens.

"Petra Kara," I read aloud. "Canadian. Nineteen. Orphan."

I scanned the bullet points on the young woman's life and immediately felt a kinship with her. My heart oozed warmth as I read the facts. She'd been raised in foster care, a straight A student, as rabid about archaeology as I had been at her age, and...

My head snapped up and I looked at Marks wide-eyed. "She's psionic?"

Marks put up a hand. "It's very light at the moment. Her therapist reports that it gives her a headache to read minds, and she can only move light items."

"Still, I don't understand how you expect to pull the wool over her eyes when she's telepathic. She'll see right through it."

Miss Marks opened the desk drawer in front of her and pulled out a dull grey pebble. She set it on the desk in front of me. "That's what we have this material for."

I picked it up, its resonance singing through my fingers like a soprano. "Wolfram?"

She nodded. "Anyone carrying this on their person will be impervious to Petra's attempts to read their mind. But it's really just a stop gap. She doesn't like to read minds and only does it when she feels it's absolutely necessary."

"Ah." I handed the metal back to her. "And why do we have to stage this dig just for her?"

Marks relaxed in her chair. "You remember I mentioned a supernatural that even Ninurta would not have been able to withstand?"

"Yes."

"That's her, if we do our job successfully."

I shot Marks a side eye. "I don't understand. She's a light psionic who gets headaches when she uses her telepathic abilities. Unless she's got something more up her sleeve..."

"Oh, but she does." Marks nodded toward the folder in my lap. "That young woman is in a class all her own. The locals would refer to her as the Euroklydon, but she'll only come fully into her abilities if we give her a little nudge in the right direction."

Euroklydon. I knew this name but it took me a moment to unearth it from the dusty back shelves of my memory. "The Euroklydon was a great wind or storm mentioned in ancient scripture, wasn't it?"

"Very good." Marks gave me another look of approval. "But she's not the Euroklydon yet, and she'll never *become* the Euroklydon unless we intervene."

"Why do it all in secret? Why not just ask her if that's what she wants and then help her turn on her powers?"

"She would never trust us if we did that. Believe me, this plan we've come up with is brilliant. It will ensure she'll trust us, and that she'll want to work with us. We've been watching her since birth, we know her personality inside and out."

Something uncomfortable niggled in my gut at these words, but I pushed it aside. Marks had been nothing but kind and supportive of me, and reporting to her was my job. I had people to support, and like she said, it was for Petra's benefit.

"Execute your part in this plan well and you'll witness something that only happens once in a generation, the birth of the most powerful supernatural the world has ever known." Jody Marks practically levitated off her chair at these words.

I couldn't stop myself from grinning. "How intriguing. Libya, here we come."

AN END AND A BEGINNING

DON'T MISS the story of Petra Kara in *Born of Air*, An Elemental Origins Novel.

**A terrifying family secret will awaken her power. Embracing it may cost Petra her life.**

All Petra Kara wants in life is to study Archaeology at the University of Cambridge. And she's so close. She's got the grades, she's got the ambition. All she needs now is an outrageous sum of money and experience on an Old World archaeological excavation. If only she could find a way to get rid of her annoying low-grade telepathy. There's nothing Petra hates more than a cheat and a liar and it's too easy to cheat when you can read people's minds.

When Petra spies an ad for a volunteer position on an excavation to North Africa, she knows its meant for her. But there is more waiting for her in Libya than broken pottery and human remains. A heart-pounding race through the desert under a sky full of stars with Jesse, her sexy dig-mate and newfound crush, ends when Petra slides into an ancient cave-system with strange stones embedded in the walls.

That's where her life changes forever.

As her powers manifest, there are those who think they have a good reason to destroy her before she becomes too powerful.

Petra knows she is far more than just gales of wind. Just how old is she? Has she lived before? Who is the man in her vision with the silver eyes? But the biggest question of all is: will she survive long enough to learn who she is and what she's really capable of?

# A.L. KNORR'S NOTES

When Ibby first came on the scene in *Born of Air*, I fell in love with her character and knew she had a much bigger story of her own to tell. Around the same time as I was penning Petra's story, which I hope you get a chance to read, I found an eager and talented writer who helped me choreograph some excellent aerial combat scenes for *The Kacy Chronicles*. I was so impressed with his work, and I was so overwhelmed by my publishing schedule at the time that I asked him if he'd be interested in co-authoring Ibby's story with me, a series I wanted to call *Rings of the Inconquo*. True to form, Aaron willingly waded into the story neck deep and leant his considerable imagination and skill to breathing life in Ibby, Uncle Iry, Marcus, Adrian Shelton, Ninurta, and all the other characters that made this series what it is.

Thank you to Aaron for being so wonderful to work with, to our editing team of Brian Cross and Nicola Aquino, to my family and my husband for your unending support, and most of all to my readers, who never seem to tire of this universe. How blessed we are.

Thank you.

Abby

# A.D. SCHNEIDER'S NOTES

It's funny that writing *Metal Angel* was coming to the end of a fantastic journey, while within the realm of the *Elemental Origins* this is just the beginning for Ibby. She still has a thrilling time ahead of herself with Petra in *Born of Air*, but for the time being my part in the story is over. Ibby, powerful and yet fragile, made of steel but oh so human, is out of my hands and into yours as she was always meant to be. A little somber maybe, but as much as I'll miss Ibby (and Marcus and Jackie and Uncle Iry) I'm walking away from this story a happy man. I'm happy because it has been nothing but great working with Mrs. Abby, who I owe so much to. I'm happy because in my own imperfect way I got to step into the world of the Elementals and tell a new story. Finally, I'm happy because I've been embraced so heartily by you, the devoted, fabulous, and numerous fans of Mrs. Abby. I may not have been able to conjure the same magic as your beloved author, but you gave me a shot at my own rugged word-weaving and made me most welcome and more than anything I hoped you enjoyed the tale I had to tell. Thank you guys.

God only knows what the future holds, but I am certain I'll keep spinning my yarns somewhere and I'm certain Mrs. Abby has nothing but more wonders by land, sea, or air for you all to enjoy. I've had the privilege of consulting on a few, and Lord willing I will again, but no matter what I am thankful to her and to you, dear readers, for investing the most precious resources any of us have; your time and your attention. Thank you again and thus I bid you farewell, *ila-laqaa'*.

-A.D. Schneider

# ACKNOWLEDGMENTS

This book and the two that proceeded it would not have been possible without so many people. First, thank you to my children and my family who had to put up with me locking myself away to hammer out another few thousand words. Your patience and support was incredible, and I am very grateful.

Next, to the editors, Mr. Cross and Nicola Aquino, whose willingness to slog through my drafts, endure my ham-fisted writing, and just general ability to find the jewels which could be polished, I give my thanks and warmest regards. I never made it easy on you, but you were always up to the task.

Of course, I can never forget the woman who is to blame for all of this. Mrs. Abby, you were willing to invest in me when I had so very little to offer, and even when there seemed so very little to show for it you kept pressing forward, lifting me up and pushing me to be better. I couldn't have asked for a better ally or a better friend, thank you.

Last and most important, to my wife, my darling and my lady. You are the one who raises my head when I'm weary, tells me fearlessly when I am wrong, and the only one who every day convinces me that the fight is worth it. You are my sparring partner, my lover, and the peg o' my heart. I can't do it without you, and I praise God every day that I have you. Thanks, babe.

-Aaron D. Schneider

## BOOKS BY A.L. KNORR

**Elemental Origins Series**

*Born of Water (Targa)*

*Born of Fire (Saxony)*

*Born of Earth (Georjayna)*

*Born of Æther (akiko)*

*Born of Air (petra)*

*The Elementals (The ensemble story)*

*The Elemental Origins Boxed Set (the Completed Series)*

**Mermaid's Return (Mira's story)**

*Returning*

*FALLING*

*Surfacing*

*Mermaid's Return, the complete box set*

**The Siren's Curse (Targa)**

*Salt & Stone*

*Salt & the Sovereign*

*Salt & the Sisters*

**Earth Magic Rises (Georjie)**

*Bones of the Witch*

*Ashes of the Wise*

*Heart of the Fae*

**Arcturus Academy (Saxony)**

*Firecracker*

*Fire Trap*

*Fire Games*

*Legends of Fire*

*Source Fire*

***The Scented Court***

*A Blossom At midnight*

*A memory of nightshade*

*A Daughter of Winter*

*A Prince of Autumn*

**The Rings of the Inconquo** (Ibby's story)

*Born of Metal*

*Metal Guardian*

*Metal Angel*

**Elemental Novellas**

*Heat, A Fire Novella*

**The Kacy Chronicles**

*Descendant*

*Ascendant*

*Combatant*

*Transcendent*

Visit www.alknorrbooks.com to sign up for A.L. Knorr's

newsletter. Get notifications for new releases and free stories.

For a complete list of stories by Aaron D Schneider, please visit www.aarondchneider.com.

Printed in Great Britain
by Amazon

38238492R00149